“You d

He smiled
gorgeous.

Eboni groaned. She was beginning to use the word *gorgeous* a bit too much.

But she couldn’t help it. His brown eyes tempted her with their warmth. They reminded her of the dark chocolate she loved to eat. The thought of nibbling on him was definitely appealing.

While his eyes were dark chocolate, his skin was like smooth caramel. She could tell that he was of mixed race. His lips, though not full, were so luscious. Her body shivered as she stared at him, and he returned her gaze.

When he moved closer and his lips covered hers, she didn’t pull away. Instead she melted into him, her lips parting to meet his onslaught.

He knew how to kiss. She could tell that much. While she hadn’t been in too many steady relationships, she’d locked lips more times than she could count and Darren ranked up there with the best.

However, something different was happening. Every nerve and fiber in her body felt as if they were alive.

She closed her eyes, savoring the unexpected feeling stirring inside. Heat coursed through her body, settling at the delicate place between her legs.

Books by Wayne Jordan

Harlequin Kimani Romance

Embracing the Moonlight
One Gentle Knight
To Love a Knight
Always a Knight
Midnight Kisses
Saved by Her Embrace
To Love You More
I'll Stand By You

WAYNE JORDAN

For as long as he can remember, Wayne Jordan loved reading, but he also enjoyed creating his own make-believe worlds. This love for reading and writing continued, and in November 2005 his first book, *Capture the Sunrise,* was published by BET Books.

Wayne has always been an advocate for romance, especially African-American romance. In 1999 he founded www.romanceincolor.com, a website that focuses on African-American romance and its authors.

Wayne is a high school teacher and a graduate of the University of the West Indies. He holds a B.A. in literature and linguistics and a M.A. in applied linguistics. He lives on the beautiful tropical island of Barbados, which, with its white sands and golden sunshine, is the perfect setting for the romance stories he loves to create. Of course, he still takes time out to immerse himself in the latest releases from his favorite authors.

I'll Stand by You

WAYNE JORDAN

HHARLEQUIN®KIMANI™ROMANCE

To my agent, Cheryl Fergusson,
whose belief in my ability and talent is unwavering,
and whose knowledge of the craft of writing helps to
transform my erratic scribbles into a thing of beauty.

Recycling programs
for this product may
not exist in your area.

ISBN-13: 978-0-373-86299-3

I'LL STAND BY YOU

Copyright © 2013 by Wayne Jordan

⊕ HARLEQUIN®

™ www.Harlequin.com

Printed in U.S.A.

Dear Reader,

I hope you enjoy *I'll Stand by You,* the first book in my new series, Once Upon a Time, which is loosely based on the fairy tales that many of us grew up listening to as we drifted off to dreamland.

With *I'll Stand By You,* I wanted to create a story about a hero, disillusioned by love, who finds the unexpected with a strong, passionate woman searching for her own knight in shining armor.

I've always wanted to tell stories, to create a world where love, romance and happily-ever-after are still important. I may no longer be a kid, but I still believe in Once Upon a Time....

Be sure to visit me at my website, www.waynejordan.net, or email me at authorwj@caribsurf.com.

May God continue to bless you.

Your friend,

Wayne Jordan

Prologue

Eboni Harrison watched as her sister Aaliyah slipped quietly into the dimly lit room. She could see that something was wrong, but she kept her focus on the tattered storybook in her hand. "And they lived happily ever after," Eboni read the story's final words.

"I want to be a princess," eight-year-old Cyndi shouted, clapping her hands in delight.

"You're already a princess." Eboni gently kissed her cheek.

As Aaliyah stepped farther into the room, everyone immediately turned in her direction.

"Where are Mommy and Daddy?" Keisha asked immediately.

Keisha, at seven years old, the youngest, sat in a corner, a doll on her lap. Usually quiet and reserved, her question was unexpected.

"Are they in Heaven?" asked Cyndi, tears in her eyes.

"Yes, they are in Heaven."

Eboni could see Aaliyah's attempt to hold back tears.

"Who's going to take care of us?" Keisha asked.

"I don't know."

"I don't want to be an orphan," Cyndi cried.

"Don't let them separate us," Keisha said.

"I can't promise you that," Aaliyah said. "I can't guarantee we won't get separated. But we have to make a promise to each other. Even if we get separated, we'll find each other," Aaliyah continued.

"Let's promise," Eboni said.

The girls moved closer together. Each of their faces positioned to cry into Aaliyah's arms.

Aaliyah held her sisters close and Eboni felt safe. Their separation was inevitable. She hoped that Keisha and Cyndi would find good families. They were beautiful and smart young girls. It didn't matter what happened to her as long as she could stay with Aaliyah.

She smiled, knowing that someday, they would have their happily-ever-after.

Chapter 1

He was downright gorgeous. No, he was more than gorgeous.

Inside, the phone rang, but she refused to move. She just wanted to feast her eyes on the hunk that was stepping out of the complex's swimming pool.

She groaned in disappointment. He wasn't wearing the tight Speedo she'd anticipated. Instead, he wore loose-fitting boxer shorts that revealed very little.

However, her eyes immediately lowered to that telltale bulge noticeable through his soaked shorts. She giggled softly.

And then, the unexpected happened. The man slipped out of the shorts and tossed them onto a pool chair. He stretched his hands in the air, and Eboni closely observed his very fitted swim trunks.

She gasped.

Lord, have mercy.

He was loaded.

She could not breathe. All she could imagine was the pleasure that he was capable of giving her.

There was an air of confidence in the way he stood, as if he knew he looked fine. There was no one at the pool, but she had no doubt that if there were people there he would have dropped the shorts with the same nonchalance as he did now.

And then he hooked his fingers in the waistband of the trunks and...stopped.

He looked in her direction and it was only then that she realized that she had gasped a second time, and he had heard.

His fingers hovered at his waist, the smile on his face blatant, daring and flirtatious.

Time stood still for a flicker of a moment, but in that moment something sparked between them.

Darren glanced up and saw the woman who lived in the condo adjacent to the one he used when he stayed nights in the city. While he owned the complex, he'd not met with her personally. His office manager had completed the sale.

She'd moved in a few weeks ago. Though she wasn't his usual type, soft and delicate, there was something about her that intrigued him. Her youthful innocence made him feel...old.

The women he usually dated were drop-dead gorgeous. Actually, all the women he was usually seen with were beautiful, but she was different. While their beauty came from a bottle or a plastic surgeon, hers appeared natural and seductive.

When he'd arrived home from work an hour ago and realized there was no one in the pool, he'd decided to take a dip. He didn't do it too often, but on nights like these, when the high-school girls who miraculously appeared whenever he went into the pool were nowhere in sight, it was safe.

He'd taken notice of his neighbor from the moment she'd appeared from behind the curtains of the glass door that led to her balcony just above the pool.

The fact that she'd been watching him furtively stroked his male pride.

On several occasions, he'd planned on walking over to her and introducing himself, but he'd decided against it. To say that he wanted her was an understatement, but wanting her didn't mean he had to have her. He prided himself on his self-control, which he'd perfected to a fine art.

His fingers were poised at the waistband of his trunks. He felt daring. At this time of night, people rarely came to the pool. He continued to stare at his neighbor and then he flicked his trunks downward.

The shock across her face was priceless. Of course, her retreating back was all he could see before he dived into the water.

Pervert! That's what he was. Eboni could feel the heat against her face.

The nerve of that man! He had no shame, no respect for the other tenants in the complex.

But the thought of him naked made her feel all tingly. How was she ever going to face him again?

She turned back, moving to the curtains and closing the door to the balcony before he saw her again. She glanced downward and realized he was focused on swimming lap after lap.

At the same time she forced herself to move, the phone rang. She wondered who it was, but then remembered. It was probably one of her brothers, checking in.

She'd only moved into the complex three weeks ago, but already her overprotective brothers were driving her crazy. She loved them, all three of them, but sometimes they took their assumed roles as her protectors a bit too seriously.

She could look back at some of their antics as humorous, but since she'd moved out of their parents' home she'd expected things to change. They had changed. Now, instead of being around all the time, her brothers made sure they dropped by every free moment they had available.

She picked up the phone. It was Maxwell, her older brother. "Hi," she said.

"Is everything all right?" he asked.

"As all right as it was yesterday when Omar called."

He ignored her comment, and continued, "You need to give Mom a call. She said that she hasn't heard from you for a few days."

"Okay, I'll give her a call," she replied abruptly. "I have to go. We'll talk later."

Before he could object, she ended the call.

She lowered herself to the couch. After such a pleasant sighting, she had to deal with this…again.

She'd hoped that her brothers would start seeing her for the independent woman she was, but their constant need to protect her was wearing thin. She'd attempted to have a serious talk with them on a few occasions, but somehow the words seemed to enter one ear and go out the other.

She glanced at the clock on the mantelpiece. Fortunately, the club was just a five-minute walk, so she'd still get there on time.

While she'd been granted leave from her full-time position as a firefighter, her classes at the fitness center, where she taught part-time, were still going on. She needed the exercise and distraction to help her deal with the loss of one of her colleagues several weeks ago.

She headed to the bedroom, hoping that a good workout with her upcoming class would clear her troubled mind.

Eboni shuffled the bags in her hand as she attempted to balance the large one. She walked slowly toward her apartment door—the hallway seemed longer than usual. She should have followed her original plan. Making two trips would have taken longer, but it would have been easier.

After what seemed like hours, she arrived at the door, the packages still balanced precariously.

She bent, put the packages down and then fumbled in the pockets of her jeans for the keys to the door.

She entered her home, placing the keys on the table

before she returned to retrieve the packages. But when she turned to step back into the apartment, she slammed into the door, not realizing it had closed behind her.

She placed the bags down and turned the door knob, and it didn't open.

An expletive she rarely used slipped with ease from her lips.

She'd locked herself out!

She fished into her pocket for the keys, hoping they were there, but remembered she'd placed them on the table beyond the door.

What the hell was she going to do?

The only spare key was at her parents' home, but to call them—or her brothers—was not an option. She'd have to go to the management company's office.

But how on earth was she going to do that, if her car keys were on her key chain?

Frustration got the best of her and she kicked one of the bags, the contents scattering across the hallway.

She watched as a can of beans rolled along the floor, slowing before it stopped between a pair of legs.

Her eyes shifted upward.

It was him.

He smiled, that lazy, probing smile that sent shivers down her spine…and farther.

"You could crawl between my legs to get it," he offered.

She snorted in disgust.

"It'll be much easier for you to move," she replied, her voice laced with sarcasm.

He laughed. "Isn't anything I say going to faze you?" he asked.

"I'm sure that nothing you say will ever faze me."

"Only what I do?" he teased again.

She blushed.

"I'm not impressed by perverts."

"Pervert? Me? I was just having a bit of fun."

"That's not what I call fun. Seeing your…" she spluttered, unable to finish what she was going to say.

"So what I do doesn't upset you, huh?" he teased, his laughter loud and hearty.

She did not respond. He picked up the can, and stepped toward her. She felt the urge to step back, but didn't. She couldn't let him see her discomfort.

When he reached her, he handed her the can. She took it cautiously.

Their fingers touched. A bolt of heat scorched her body.

Their eyes met, each probing the other.

She was the first to look away, his gaze too intense.

"How can I help you?" he asked, his voice low and concerned.

"I'm fine," she replied.

"So why are you standing out here kicking your belongings around? Let's put our very memorable introduction aside and start over."

Again, she did not respond, but she did notice the mockery was gone.

"I locked myself out," she finally responded. "My keys are inside."

"Spare?"

"At my parents'."

"I could take you there to get it, but the building manager's office is just a few blocks away. You could go there. I'm sure they will have a spare."

"My car keys are on the same bunch," she acknowledged. She was sure that by now he was thinking that she was quite foolish.

"I'll take you," he said.

Though she was skeptical, she knew she had no choice.

"Thanks for offering."

He seemed surprised at her response, but he quickly regained his composure.

"Come, the office is not too far. It won't take us long to get there."

"Thanks again."

He smiled briefly and turned to leave. She followed.

Outside, she followed him to a steel-blue Ferrari.

The fit was perfect. He looked like the Ferrari type— daring and adventurous with a bit of arrogance.

He opened the door for her, waiting until she was seated and comfortable. Not that she could ever feel comfortable around him.

Closing the door, he circled the car and took his seat. Soon, they were on the street.

"I don't know your name," he said, breaking the silence. "I'm Darren Grayson."

"I'm Eboni Wynter."

She waited for the laughter or a smile, but when neither came she relaxed. Her name had often become the butt of most people's jokes.

"Well, Ms. Wynter, it's a pleasure to finally meet you. I noticed you only moved in a few weeks ago. I hope you can forgive me for my little indiscretion the other night."

"It didn't bother me much," she lied.

"Sure," he said. "If that's the way you want to deal with it."

Before she could respond, he pulled the car to the entrance of the manager's office.

"I'll wait here for you, so I don't need to park."

He searched in his pocket and pulled his wallet out, tossing her a few bills. "I suspect you're going to have to pay some sort of inconvenience fee for the lockout," he said.

She hesitated, but took the money anyway. She didn't have a choice, but being indebted to anyone wasn't a good feeling.

"And here is my ID. Just let them know I'm vouching for you. I've been living in the complex for a while, so they know me."

"Thanks," she replied, taking the card. "I'll be sure to pay you back."

"A few dollars won't leave me broke. It's not every day that I get to help a damsel in distress."

She stepped from the car, glad to be away from the stifling confines and the close proximity to Darren.

She proceeded into the building and in five minutes she was out again, his twenty-dollar loan in the office's coffers.

When he saw her, he smiled, a smile she'd already

grown accustomed to. The smile was in keeping with his witty, laid-back personality.

She opened the door and stepped into the car, showing him the key she'd had to purchase.

"Good, you had enough money."

She nodded, handing him the bills she'd not used.

"I don't know how to thank you."

"A home-cooked meal would be fine," he replied, laughter in his eyes.

"Sure," she responded casually. She didn't think he was serious anyway.

"So what about tonight?" he asked.

She turned her head to face him as he started the car and pulled onto the street.

"You're serious?" she asked.

"Of course I am. Why would you think I'm not?"

"Don't know. Maybe it's the way you said it."

"The way I said it?"

She paused, trying to find the right words.

"Cat got your tongue?" he teased.

"I'm generally not at a loss for words, but you seem to have this strange effect on me," she admitted.

"I do seem to have an effect on women," he replied. There was no trace of pride or arrogance in his voice. He'd said it with the confidence of a man who knew who he was and didn't need to boast.

"So, how about dinner? If you can't cook, that's fine. You can order pizza. I don't want you for your cooking. Just your body."

She stared at him, not sure if he was being serious or poking fun at her. But his eyes twinkled and he laughed.

His smile disappeared when he noticed her serious expression.

"I'm sorry. I know I can be annoying at times," he admitted. "But I do want to have dinner with you. Just dinner," he repeated.

When he stepped into her condo fifteen minutes later, she could tell that he was impressed by what he saw.

She'd decorated her new home just how she wanted it. It was an artistic blend of contemporary and classic that had somehow come together. She hoped it reflected her personality.

"I like," he said, nodding his appreciation, "very much."

"I'm surprised," she replied. "I didn't expect you to be the artistic type."

"I studied art in college."

His admission was a surprise but she was sure that his interest in art had nothing to do with his job.

"So what do you do for a living?" he asked.

She hesitated briefly before she answered. "I'm a firefighter."

He whistled loudly, surprising her with his enthusiastic reaction. It felt strange. Men didn't usually react to her career choice that way. In fact, most of them would have already raced out the door.

"That's awesome," he said. "That's what I wanted to be when I was growing up. It must be fascinating!"

"Sometimes, but it's hard work."

"Your parents must be really supportive. My mom

would have given birth to a cow if I'd attempted to do something like that."

"I assure you, mine were not at all enthused when I made the announcement. It took a while for them to accept my decision, but they have been really supportive ever since. They've always told us that we must go after our own dreams."

"I'm sure they regretted making that statement."

"You don't know the half of it."

"You said *us*. You have brothers and sisters?"

"Just brothers. Three, in fact," she replied. "I also call them my jailors. They are obsessed with protecting me."

"What's wrong with them wanting to protect you?" he asked.

"I have no problem with them being brothers, but when it goes to the extreme, it becomes a problem. Since my twin brothers decided to study in New York, they're still at home and are driving me crazy. Maxwell, fortunately, moved out when he got married, but he, too, can be a bit too protective of all of us. That's the main reasons I finally had to move out. I needed my independence and my own space."

"You do seem to be a strong woman... I like that."

He smiled, nodding his approval. His eyes were gorgeous.

Eboni groaned. She was beginning to use the word *gorgeous* a bit too much.

But she couldn't help it. His brown eyes tempted her with their warmth. They reminded her of the dark chocolate she loved to eat. The thought of nibbling on him was definitely appealing.

While his eyes were dark chocolate, his skin was like smooth caramel. She could tell that he was of mixed race. His lips, though not full, were so luscious. Her body shivered as she stared at him, and he returned her gaze.

When he moved closer and his lips covered hers, she didn't pull away. Instead, she melted into him, her lips parting to meet his onslaught.

He knew how to kiss. She could tell that much. While she hadn't been in too many steady relationships, she'd locked lips more times that she could count, and Darren ranked up there with the best.

However, something different was happening. Every nerve and fiber in her body tingled.

She closed her eyes, savoring the unexpected feeling stirring inside. Heat coursed through her body, settling at the delicate place between her legs.

Darren lifted her blouse. Cool air tightened her already erect nipples. He lowered his head, sucking briefly on one nipple before he tugged it gently between his teeth, causing her to call his name. He did the same with the other dusky orb and she moaned her pleasure.

When he raised his head, an intense ache assaulted her, and she then sighed her disappointment.

Again, he captured her lips, and her hands reached for the bulge in his pants.

In the distance, bells began to ring and she wondered if she was hearing things.

His body moved from against hers, startling her out of the moment.

It was the doorbell. She scrambled up immediately,

pulling her blouse down and breathing in deeply in an attempt to calm herself.

Darren rose to his feet, his own breathing erratic.

"Are you expecting someone?" he managed to ask.

"No, but I have an idea who's at the door."

"I'll leave," he responded, nodding his understanding.

"No, wait," she said quickly. She then tidied herself enough to walk over to the door and slowly open it.

Chapter 2

Eboni never failed to be amazed at the beauty of her brothers and her love for all three of them.

However, the two facing her, Kemar and Omar, the twins, did not inspire love in her at the moment.

"What are you doing here?" she demanded. "I thought we'd agreed that you call before you dropped by."

"I know we did. But Omar and I were just in the neighborhood, so we knew our darling sister wouldn't mind if we just dropped by."

She snorted. "Just in the neighborhood, huh? So what were you doing around here?"

They did not respond; however, their eyes focused on Darren. Invisible arrows soared in his direction. And for Darren, they were definitely invisible. He seemed totally unconcerned with their presence. It fact, he seemed annoyed about the interruption.

"Who's he?" Omar asked, motioning with his head in Darren's direction.

Darren stood when she did not respond.

"I'm Eboni's next-door neighbor," he politely responded.

He stepped forward and put his hand out in greeting, but lowered it when they just stood looking at him.

Eboni seethed.

"There's no need to be impolite," she said. "You're in my home now."

They had the decency to look embarrassed.

"Sorry," they said in unison.

"We didn't mean to be rude," Omar said.

"It was just a surprise to find someone here," Kemar said, his expression childishly repentant. "Eboni is sort of a loner." He lifted the bag in his hand. "We brought donuts for her. She has a sweet tooth."

She grabbed for the bag and opened it immediately, savoring the smell of her favorite, honey-glazed éclairs. The fact that they'd brought donuts for her lessened her anger.

When she glanced up, she realized her brothers had moved closer to Darren.

The interrogation was about to begin.

She watched her brothers, as she always did, with a mixture of dread and admiration.

Omar, the journalist-to-be, moved in slowly, while Kemar, the budding psychologist, sent question after question Darren's way.

However, there was something different about this situation. While they continued their questioning, little did they realize that the tables had been turned and that they were now answering Darren's questions.

Darren yawned. While he had remained tolerant, she could see he had finally had enough.

"Well, gentlemen, I really don't want to be rude but I have to be going. It was nice to meet you, *boys*. I'm sure I'll see you around."

His statement and its meaning were clear. He had every intention of dropping by again.

He turned to Eboni and smiled. "We'll have to continue were we left off."

Her brothers' eyes widened, but they said nothing, seeming still bemused by the ineffectiveness of their mission.

Eboni followed him to the door, watching as he opened it and walked out.

Before she could close the door behind him, he turned.

"I mean it. We're going to continue where we left off."

With that he bent his head and then placed the softest of kisses on her lips before turning to walk away.

Closing the door softly, Eboni turned toward her brothers, not surprised to see the accusations in their eyes.

She threw caution to the wind. Her anger boiled below the surface.

"I think it's time for the two of you to leave. This is

the last time you'll drop by without letting me know, or I'll refuse to let you in."

"You can't do that," Omar countered, his eyes sparking with fire.

"I can't? Just you wait and see, bro. This is my home and you won't be coming here unless I invite you."

She turned her back to them, walking purposely toward the door, then opened it wide and waited for them to follow.

At first, they did not move, but realizing she was serious, they headed reluctantly to the door.

When they reached the door, she whispered the words she always did.

"I love you."

They turned to her, their expressions softening as they repeated her sentiment.

She pushed them out the door, not waiting to see them retreat.

Her anger had dissipated, but her frustration was still present. She wondered if their overprotectiveness was ever going to stop.

Maybe when she got married, but she would have to first reach that step, and the way her brothers protected her, there was little prospect of her meeting anyone she liked enough who could tolerate them.

But Darren had dealt with them and with confidence. She could not help but admire the way he'd handled the situation.

She smiled.

Yes, if there was anyone whom she needed in her life right now it may be him.

Darren closed the door as he stepped into his condo.

He wanted to laugh out loud at what had just happened, but his empathy for his next-door neighbor reduced the humor.

Her brothers were obviously a trip, so he could see why she'd purchased the condo.

He'd acquired the massive complex several years ago and done extensive renovations, including adding a pool and underground parking, which had taken his designers hours of work, but the end result had been exactly as he'd visualized it.

When one of the condos had gone up for sale, he'd been skeptical about the young lady who'd wanted to purchase, but his lawyer had assured him that she had the money and when he did his own trace of her, he'd discovered that her parents were quite wealthy.

From the first time he'd seen her, his attraction to her had been intense. To say she'd had an impact on him would be an understatement.

While he did use this condo on occasion, he didn't use it too often. Usually, he'd head to his home in Scarsdale following a day in the office. Recently, however, he'd been coming back each night, hoping to get a glimpse of her. On his way to the shower, the phone rang.

He picked it up, smiling when he saw his ex-wife's number on the display.

"Daddy, I've been calling you all evening."

"Sorry, honey. You don't usually call me during the week."

"I know, but I was just calling to remind you about Parents' Day on Monday. Are you still coming on Saturday, so you can spend the weekend?"

"I didn't forget, honey. And, yes, I'll be there for the whole weekend."

"That's what you said last time, Dad."

"That's true, but I promise I won't miss this one."

"All of the other kids will have their daddies there. I just want you to be there, too."

"I will, honey. Now you go off to sleep. It is way past your bedtime."

"I'm going to bed now. Mommy just finished reading to me and told me it was okay to call."

"Well, off to bed now. I'll call your mom tomorrow."

"I love you, Daddy."

"I love you, honey bunny."

Kenya laughed as she always did when he called her by her pet name.

"Sleep tight and don't let the bedbugs bite," he whispered softly.

She laughed again, and this time a loud yawn followed.

Darren heard the soft click and the call disconnected.

He felt empty inside whenever he talked to his daughter. She was the only reason he hated the divorce. His ex-wife, Barbara, had won custody of Kenya and since she'd remarried and moved to Baltimore, he didn't get

to see Kenya except for holidays, some weekends and
during her summer recess. Of course, when she'd asked
him to come to her school, he'd immediately agreed.
He couldn't refuse his daughter anything. He missed
her and going to Baltimore meant he'd get a chance to
spend the entire weekend with her.

He rose from the bed, deciding to try the shower
once more. He didn't want to think about what had happened in the past. It was too late to do anything about
it anymore. He needed to focus on the present and the
future. Being divorced didn't automatically mean that
he was a failure with relationships. He just needed to
find the right woman.

The next evening, Eboni lay in bed listening to the
faint hum of traffic on the outside. She loved this part
of the Upper East Side, away from the chaos of the
city center. It was not that she didn't like the hustle and
bustle of city life, but she'd wanted her home to be in
a relatively quiet neighborhood and she'd been lucky.
While the noise increased during the day, at night only
the occasional honking of a passing vehicle disturbed
the relatively peaceful neighborhood.

She reached automatically for the photo in the drawer
next to the bed.

It was black and white and had turned yellow with
age.

The photo had been taken just before the accident. It
was one of those Sundays her family had spent in Pros-

pect Park. Their weekly Sunday picnic, as her mother used to call it.

She traced a finger along the photo, touching her sisters, willing them to be near. Fourteen years ago they'd been separated. Initially, she'd missed them, but as the years passed she'd put aside any hope of seeing them again. But a year ago, she'd decided that she had to know. She'd hired a private investigator, but, so far, every lead had taken him nowhere.

But she had no intentions of giving up hope. While she'd put the memories of her sisters behind her for years, coming of age had made her long for other things, especially her sisters. While she had no doubt that her brothers loved her, she often ached for a sisterly bond. She did have a best friend at work, Cheryl, but that did little to diminish her need for her sisters.

Growing up she'd never worried about being lonely. Her brothers had always been there for her, carrying her with them to games and, on occasion, their dates. Fortunately, most of their female friends had thought she was adorable.

She loved her brothers. But at twenty-four, their obsession with protecting her was getting a bit tired. They were all single, handsome young men, but they needed to focus on their own relationships, not her.

And none of them were in a serious relationship. In fact, her brothers seemed so focused on sowing their wild oats that their mother seemed to have given up hope that they would ever marry.

Her thoughts eased back to her handsome, sexy

neighbor. Maybe the only way to keep her brothers at bay was to find a boyfriend whom her parents would approve of. Her brothers would have no choice but to fall in line.

She examined the characteristics about Darren that would put him in their favor.

He was handsome and appeared wealthy. While her parents were not snobs, they knew that their affluence and her own personal trust fund made her a target for predators. Not that she had any problem with finding male friends. She was attractive and handled a career most women couldn't even begin to fathom. Now her life was becoming a bit more complicated.

Darren was the first male in a long time that she'd felt attracted to. There was something about him that made her feel hot inside. Anxious, hot, wet…he made her feel all those things and more.

In her bedroom, she slipped on her silk bathrobe as soon as her bath was over.

Since she'd moved in, the boredom of inactivity was making her crazy. But taking leave from work had not been a choice. For days after, and even now, the memory of the cries of her dying coworker had kept her awake. Thankfully, she'd slept better for the past few nights. Guilt, like a sudden downpour, washed over her.

She turned off the lights, closed her eyes and embraced the darkness.

The weekend passed with very little activity. She did her personal-training hours at the health club on

Friday and spent much of the weekend reading. Saturday night, on the spur of the moment, she decided to use the Broadway ticket she'd received for her birthday. The mood and tone of *The Lion King* was just what she needed to keep her mind off the man whose image seemed to constantly haunt her dreams at night.

On Sunday morning when she woke, she saw that her brother Maxwell had called and left a message. He wanted her to meet him at Roberta's, her favorite pizzeria, for lunch. She knew the reason for his invitation, but Maxwell knew exactly how to tempt her. The temptation was too great to refuse.

Maxwell, her oldest brother, was the conservative accountant. With one failed marriage under his belt, he believed he was the expert on marriage, giving his younger siblings advice even when they didn't want it.

Of course, he encouraged his younger brothers to sow their wild oats before committing to a life of "loss of self-identity and nagging." He had often used these words to describe his own marriage.

Just before midday, Eboni walked into the restaurant and followed the hostess to where Maxwell sat, immaculately dressed in a starched white shirt and dark blue suit.

As always she was struck by how handsome he was. It was ironic that his personality complemented his physical appearance.

He was just over six feet tall, his skin a smooth mahogany like that of his brothers. However, that was where the resemblance ended. While Omar and Kemar favored their father, Maxwell favored their mother. His hair, a source of annoyance, was inclined to be a bit too curly. However, after years of trying to tame it into submission, he'd finally given up. What the hair did, however, was add a touch of chaos to an image that was almost anally immaculate.

Always the perfect gentleman, he stood when she reached the table where he sat. He hugged her and she felt the warmth that he seemed to reserve only for his family. Then he smiled, transforming his usually stoic face into a thing of beauty.

"Thanks for coming, sis."

She smiled in return. It was not easy to be angry with her brothers. She knew they loved her and maybe that should be enough for her. But she wanted more. She wanted them to respect her and her choices.

He waited, like the gentleman he was, until she sat, before he took his seat.

She smiled when he ordered Roberta's Grapefruit Basil Soda for her, a light beer for himself and a large Speckenwolf pizza, her favorite, for the both of them to share. Lunch was going to be interesting. He was definitely piling on the charm.

"So how has the move to the new digs been?" he asked.

The use of the word *digs* was so out of character for Maxwell, she found herself smiling.

"My *digs* are fine," she replied.

A single eyebrow rose at her teasing, but he didn't say anything.

"I'm glad you like it. At least it's in a suitable neighborhood," he commented.

"And if it weren't?" she asked. She could almost hear his response, but she didn't care. The reason for this lunch date was obvious to her now. It was a matter of time before he lectured her.

"So that's the way you want to handle this?" he replied stiffly.

"I'm not sure what you mean," she said coyly.

"You know exactly what I mean," he replied with a calmness that didn't quite reach his eyes.

She didn't react. It was better to wait to hear what he had to say.

"Since you know why I wanted to meet you, I'll get straight to the point. Omar and Kemar told me that they paid you a visit a few nights ago." She could already hear the censure in his voice.

"Yes. They did. Of course, they didn't have the manners to call and say they were dropping by."

"I didn't realize we would need to call if we planned on dropping by," he said, fiddling with his napkin.

"Now you know," she stated firmly. "I think it's just common courtesy to do so."

"I'll remember that if I decide to stop in." He nodded his agreement, but she could hear the sarcasm in his voice.

"Maybe I'll just send an invitation when I want visitors," she retorted.

"Yes, you should. I'm sure I wouldn't want the kind of embarrassment your brothers had to endure."

"As I said, if they'd called they would not have had to endure embarrassment. I couldn't help but be embarrassed by their almost childish behavior."

"You should have been the one to be embarrassed," he stated. "That time of night and a man in your home."

"And good sex, too," she blurted out.

On reflection, she should not have used the *S* word, but Maxwell's behavior was a bit too much. She wanted to laugh, but held back when she saw the expression on his face.

"Do you know who he is?" Matthew asked.

"Who?"

"Darren Grayson."

"He's my next-door neighbor."

"He may be, but he's not the kind of man you should be hanging out with."

She could not believe he had the audacity to say that.

"Since I'm no longer a little girl, I think I can hang out with whomever I want to," she stated as calmly as she could.

"Then don't come running to me when you get hurt. Darren Grayson may be one of New York's most eligible bachelors, and own one of the wealthiest real estate companies, but he's a playa and has no problem bedding any women who catches his fancy."

"I think it's about time I go," she said, rising from her seat. She dismissed the waitress who'd just arrived with their drinks.

"I'm sure my brother doesn't need to drink that. He's already drunk."

She turned to Maxwell.

"I'll talk to you later," she said, her voice more controlled that she felt.

With that she smiled and walked away, not looking back to see the stunned expression she knew she'd find on Maxwell's face.

For the first time, she felt as if she had won a small victory.

Eboni awoke to the sounds of the city. She'd not slept well. Maxwell had tried to reach her last night but she'd refused to answer. She'd had enough of her brothers and had every intention of calling her parents to let them know what was going on. While her mother had been supportive of her move, her father had been pretty reluctant. However, once they'd seen the condo she'd purchased, she knew they'd felt more comfortable with her move. Of course, her dad would have loved her to stay in the house forever, but she'd told him firmly, "That's never going to happen." As expected he'd broken into loud laughter, one of the things she loved most about him.

She couldn't imagine a life without them, and while memories of her birth parents were still present, their images were no longer as strong, though she knew they would always be a part of her life.

She loved her parents.

When they'd visited the orphanage, those many years ago, she'd been angry and scared. Angry that the Wynters were taking her away from the only sister she had left at the orphanage, and afraid because she hadn't known what the future would hold.

But things had turned out just right. From the night she'd moved into her new home, she'd fallen in love with her three brothers. They'd just returned home from summer camp, in time to meet their new sister. She'd been unsure that night, but within an hour's time her new brothers had taken her under their wings.

She'd reveled in the warmth of their love. They'd become her brothers, but they'd also become her friends.

She glanced down at her watch and realized it was time to get to the health club to teach her class. She loved this special Monday class with children with special needs. She'd launched the program just over a year ago, and already they'd added two additional classes. She'd happily added those classes to her schedule, but when she returned to being a firefighter, she knew she wouldn't have enough time to devote to each class.

As she dressed, her thoughts strayed to Darren. She'd not seen him since last week and, as his car was missing, wondered if he'd gone away. Maybe he was with one of the many girlfriends Maxwell had told her about.

She pushed the thoughts from her mind. She couldn't let what Maxwell had said affect her impressions of Darren. In time, she would discover all she needed to know about him. She refused to be clouded by other, more public impressions of him. She would make her own decision.

She shook her head, dismissing any further thoughts.

She needed to get to class. She quickly grabbed her gym bag and headed for the door.

On Monday afternoon, Darren kissed his daughter goodbye.

As he walked down the cobblestone path, he glanced back, knowing that she'd be at the window, blowing kisses at him. He laughed when she appeared, and blew her the kiss he knew she was expecting.

He'd enjoyed the weekend in Baltimore and had clapped with pride when Kenya had made her presentation. He wished she lived with him, but his ex-wife was a much better mother than he was a father. He'd allowed his work to get in the way of his marriage and he'd had to suffer the consequences. Fortunately, things had changed. He'd once considered fighting for custody of his daughter, but he soon realized how unfair it would be to Kenya, separating her from her familiar surroundings and everything she knew. He knew that she deserved better than that.

He'd quickly given his ex-wife custody, but only under the condition that while Kenya didn't live with him, she would still spend part of each year's school vacation with him. Barbara had agreed.

Their first holiday together had been last year. The first days had been tentative ones. He'd cleared his calendar and taken two weeks holiday—one they had spent at his home, the other at Walt Disney World and Universal Studios. He had finally connected with her.

Her "I love you, Dad" when he'd dropped her back to her mother's home had almost broken him.

He'd vowed at the time that he'd never let anything come between him and his daughter again. So far, he'd kept his word.

He glanced at his watch. It would take him at least four hours to get back to home. He could stay the night, but he wanted to get back to Manhattan. He had to confess to himself that his next-door neighbor intrigued him. Even now he ached to see her. The kisses they'd shared had not been enough for him. He wanted more, much more.

As had become the norm, her image wormed itself into his consciousness.

He shook his head, willing himself back to the task of driving.

When he turned the radio on, the music of the late Bob Marley filled the car.

From the time his music teacher at high school had introduced him to the Jamaican reggae artist, he'd fallen in love with the strong pulsating beat of the music. Over the years, his connection with the music had become lost, but with the release of the documentary *Marley,* he'd purchased a greatest-hits album and had fallen in love all over again.

When he arrived in Manhattan, the sun was setting, the lights of the city slowly flickering on.

He parked his car in the designated spot, noticing that Eboni's silver Lexus was also parked.

As soon as he took a shower, he planned on inviting

himself over again. Hopefully, memories of his kiss would be enough to get him in the door.

As he stepped out of his car, he felt the motion of someone coming toward him.

He closed the car door and turned around.

Eboni.

He breathed deeply.

She stared at him.

He breathed deeply again.

All he could think of was her unclothed body in his bed.

It should be illegal for her to wear the short shorts and tank top that cupped her breasts in a way he wanted to.

He felt the first hint of arousal and tried not to stare. He noticed the Nike logo on her sneakers, before his gaze moved upward again.

"Hi," she finally said.

"Hi," he echoed.

She looked at him strangely, before she said, "I haven't seen you in a few days." He could hear a trace of accusation.

"Sorry, I was away on a personal matter," he said.

Eboni nodded, but her eyes remained expressionless. He felt a sharp disappointment at her lack of enthusiasm, but knew he had to take the blame. He didn't know how to make this right.

"I am sorry, I didn't tell you I was leaving town for the weekend," he said, walking over to stand before her. "I had an engagement."

He noticed the stiffness in her relax.

"I'm going to make dinner when I go up. Running makes me hungry. Want to join me?" Her voice followed him.

"Is that an invitation to dinner?" he asked.

"Yes. Unless you are too tired from traveling."

"I'm fine. Just need to take a bath."

"Give me an hour, before you come over—that should give you enough time," she said and headed into the building.

Darren watched as she walked away, admiring the sway of her hips.

How the hell did she get into those shorts?

Chapter 3

Eboni tossed the salad and placed it in the refrigerator. Her hands were trembling. To say she was excited to have Darren over was an understatement.

She wanted him with an intensity that she could not understand. Even now her body burned in anticipation of what would come, or at least what she hoped would come.

On the stove, fish fillets sautéed while fluffy potatoes baked in the oven. The meal would be simple, but she knew that whatever she cooked would be good. Her mother had taught her well, and while she and her brothers had been allowed to run wild, their mother had insisted they learn to cook.

Although she, Omar and Kemar were very good in the kitchen, Maxwell was the best. His culinary skills never ceased to amaze her.

There was a knock on the door and she glanced up at the clock above the refrigerator, its minute hand moving silently upward.

She took the apron from around her waist, placed it over a nearby stool and headed to the door. He was just on time.

When she opened the door, the impact of his appearance nearly knocked her backward, and she again wondered how a man could be so blatantly sexy.

"I hope I'm not too early, but I don't like to be late, especially when it's an invitation from a beautiful woman," he said, a broad smile on his face.

"No, it's fine. I'm almost done. Come in."

"Good, I'm starving," he replied, rubbing his stomach. "Fast food is not my idea of good eating, so the stop I made on my drive back didn't encourage me to eat much. One greasy burger was enough."

"Oh, dear," she exclaimed. "I made burgers." She giggled, noticing the brief look of despair.

"Just teasing," she laughed. "I can assure you, burgers will rarely be on my menu when I invite you over."

"That's good to know," he commented. "Though a juicy grilled burger is definitely preferred over the fast-food-restaurant style."

"I can promise you those," she said.

He walked in, his body brushing hers, and immediately she tingled with a flash of heat. She stopped briefly, willing her body under control, but he seemed oblivious to her reaction.

She led him to the sitting room, where she gestured to the sofa.

"I'll be back in five," she said, before she excused herself and headed back to the kitchen.

Darren didn't sit, but stood watching Eboni as she disappeared. He was going to need all the self-control he could muster.

Each time he saw her, he couldn't fail to be impressed with the difference in style. She never looked the same. Well, except that each time he saw her she oozed sexiness. He was sure she didn't even realize how sexy she was.

But while the attraction was there, he needed to be cautious. He didn't want to find himself in a situation that had the potential for disaster.

Her brothers were reason enough to run in the other direction.

But his reaction to her scared him a bit. Memories of his failed marriage surfaced again. But there was something about Eboni that felt different. With his past relationships, at the start he'd always felt in charge and in control.

With Eboni he felt vulnerable, as if she were the one in charge. He'd never felt this kind of confusion and it concerned him.

The sound of soft footsteps made him turn his head in her direction.

"Can you help me put the plates on the table?" she asked. "I have to go back to the kitchen."

"Want me to go get them?" he asked politely.

Eboni shook her head. "I'll get them. You *do* know how to set the table?" she asked, laughter in her voice.

"Of course I do," he said.

"Good."

Within a few moments she returned and handed him the plates she was carrying and headed back out the door.

He added the plates and dishes to what was already on the table.

His stomach growled appreciatively at the distinct aroma.

Eboni walked into the room just as he'd completed his task. She placed the few food dishes on the table and asked him to sit.

He complied, noticing she'd placed him opposite her, instead of the chair next to her.

While he was sure she was trying to avoid touching him, little did she realize that sitting across from her allowed him to look directly at her during dinner.

At first the conversation was awkward—strange since they'd talked about everything under the sun the first night they were together. He'd enjoyed her company that night, but tonight, he suspected something was on her mind.

He placed his knife and fork down, and decided to bite the bullet.

"Before we go any further tonight," he said, his gaze meeting hers, "tell me what's wrong."

She looked at him, almost startled by his comment.

"There is nothing wrong," she said. He noticed the lightest hesitation.

"That's not completely true," she continued. "I was

annoyed that you left without letting me know, and—"
She paused.

"And…?" he prompted.

"I really don't want to upset you."

"I'll be fine. I'm a big boy."

"My oldest brother, Maxwell, did some research on you and went on to tell me what he found out."

"Not that I am surprised, but I would have thought you'd do your own research."

"That's true. I was tempted to look you up, but decided to go the traditional way. However, I noticed that you're wealthy." She thought of his luxury car and tailored clothes.

"And that's a problem? You must be a bit wealthy, too, or you wouldn't be living here." He chuckled.

"Well, my parents are. I used part of my trust fund to purchase this condo, but my work and the part-time classes I teach at the health club take care of my everyday expenses. I do not want to touch the rest of my trust fund until it's absolutely necessary."

He looked at her closely and he noticed something he'd not seen before. There was a confidence and strength in her eyes that spoke volumes. Yet there was also a hint of uncertainty.

Her brothers.

He could tell she fought long and hard to achieve a measure of independence and from what he'd seen the other night, Eboni still had a long way to go before her brothers accepted the inevitability of their little sister so much as dating.

"So what's for dessert?" he asked, changing the conversation abruptly. The drift of their talk was going in a direction he didn't want, bringing back too many painful memories.

Tonight, for sure, he'd been thinking about all the mistakes he'd made…and his loneliness.

"Yes, which do your prefer," she asked, "cheesecake or ice cream?"

"Both," he said

Eboni laughed aloud. "How did I know that that was what you were going to say?"

"It is a compliment to your cooking. Not everyone cooks to my standard and I have a good standard. I don't eat just anything."

She rose from her chair. He wondered if she realized the double entendre in his words. He'd always been very selective, and Eboni Wynter was definitely worthy to be on his plate.

"I'll be back with the dessert," she said.

He paused for a moment, watching the sway of her backside as she walked out of the room.

He rose from his chair, glad she was gone. His erection strained against the zipper of his pants, the discomfort slowly causing his erection to return to its flaccid state.

Minutes later, when she returned, she was carrying two large bowls with generous slices of cheesecake, topped with two scoops of strawberry ice cream.

She handed him a bowl and placed hers on the table.

"What's your pleasure?" she said, nodding her head toward a state-of-the-art stereo system.

"I'm not picky, but I love reggae, some hip-hop, a bit of country, Darius Rucker, of course."

"All of my favorites," she said. She seemed pleased. "The fact that Rucker is sexy and knows how to seduce a woman with music does have its appeal."

A stab of jealously startled him. He didn't much like her talking about other men. He wanted her to focus on him.

Eboni placed her bowl on the table and walked over to the stereo. Soon, the strains of Rucker's "Come Back Song" filled the room.

She turned to Darren and held out her hand.

He stood, walking slowly over to her. When he reached her, she stepped into his arms. He held her close, enjoying the feeling of her body next to his.

At first, he swayed to the music, feeling the words and the rhythm, but slowly things changed. He became more aware of her. Her softness and her heat.

He could tell she wanted him, and his growing erection was evidence enough that he wanted her.

Her body pushed against his, and he did all he could to stifle the moan that threatened to escape his lips.

What the hell was he doing?

He was falling into the same trap as he had with women before her.

He took his arms from around her, stepping back suddenly.

His mind registered the startled look on her face, but his only goal was to get as far away from Eboni as possible.

"Thanks for dinner, but I have to go."

He turned and walked out of the kitchen, knowing that she would follow.

At the door, he turned to her.

"I'm sorry," he said softly.

All she did was stare at him. He noticed the water pooling in her eyes, and he knew with a greater certainty that he had to go and immediately. He would only hurt this beautiful woman who wanted love. He was no good for her.

He opened the door and stepped outside, refusing to look back.

Darren slammed the door behind him, and immediately headed to his bedroom. He stripped his clothes off, and slid between the sheets. He knew sleep would not come easily.

He still wasn't sure what had just happened. When he'd gone over to Eboni's apartment, he'd planned to let nature take its course.

But he realized something in that moment. He liked Eboni...and liked her a lot, which in turn made him afraid.

His initial feelings had been all physical, but spending time in her company made him realize that there was more to his feelings than the physical.

And he liked kissing her. Even now, his body burned from the heat of their contact.

He knew she wanted something more than casual and, for that reason, he'd walked away. He knew he'd hurt her. The tears in her eyes had almost broken his heart, but he'd forced himself to walk away. Though, he'd done it for the best. He was not the marrying kind and Eboni definitely was.

Since his divorce, he'd played the field without concern for anyone but himself. He'd chosen his lovers carefully—career women who didn't want marriage. These women were satisfied with a rich man to escort them to functions and great sex, and he provided both.

With that lifestyle, he'd achieved a reputation. No wonder Eboni's brother had warned her about him. If she had any sense, she'd heed her brother's words and run in the other direction when she saw him coming.

Even now, he thought about the baggage he'd brought from his past marriage and realized that had played a serious part in its failure.

For years, he'd been driven by work and making money. He had lots and lots of it, but still he drove himself to get more. At age thirty-two, he could probably retire, hire people to run the company and live for the rest of his life maintaining the same standard of living.

He was proud of the company he'd built. With two offices in New York, one close to his condo complex and another one downtown, he'd achieved way more than he'd expected.

In the process of reaching his goals, he'd ignored his wife and daughter. For a while, Barbara had been happy, but then, the dissatisfaction of being at home all day had taken its toll and she'd retuned to work. From that point, their marriage had spiraled out of control.

One thing he did eventually realize was that he hadn't taken the time to get to know his wife.

Ironically, in just a few days, he felt as though he

knew Eboni better than he'd known Barbara after five years of marriage.

Already he missed her, missed her so badly.

In the silence of the room, he laughed out loud. He couldn't stay away from her. He knew that as much as he knew the sun would rise the next day. Even now he ached to be with her.

He loved it when he was with her. How she made him laugh. How he couldn't keep his eyes off of her.

He sighed. Tomorrow was another day. After work, he'd pay her a visit and make things right.

Eboni continued to stare at the television, oblivious to the changing images. She wasn't sure what she was watching. All she could see was Darren's back as he retreated from her condo.

She had thought all day about making love with him and, while she'd been disappointed, she was more concerned about his reaction. She knew something was wrong. He just needed to trust her enough to tell her what it was.

One of the things she'd discovered about love was that trust took precedence above all.

Chapter 4

Eboni heard a knock and, knowing it was Darren, opened the door. "What do you want?" she asked, frustration apparent in her tone.

"May I come in?"

"Doesn't matter what you have to say."

"I know you're angry with me, but I'd prefer not to talk in the hallway."

She was about to respond with a sharp retort, but realized she was being rather childish.

"Okay, you have five minutes."

"Thanks. I probably don't deserve so much," he said as he entered.

She didn't respond. Instead, she closed the door, turned and walked toward the living room. Darren followed, the sound of his footsteps sure and determined behind her. She stopped when she reached the sofa and, after he took a seat, she moved to sit opposite him.

If he noticed her deliberate attempt to not sit next to him, he didn't show it.

When she sat down, he fixed his gaze on her. She felt a bit disconcerted but tried her best to remain cool and calm.

"I want to apologize for last night."

She didn't say anything. She wasn't going to make it easy for him.

"And I'd like to be as honest as I can be."

She nodded, her first acknowledgment that she was listening.

"I like you. I really like you," he confessed. "Last night, I wanted to make love to you." He paused.

"But that wasn't the problem," he continued. "My feelings for you extend beyond sex and that scares the hell out of me. I'm not proud of it, but for the past few years, I've gained somewhat of a reputation. And maybe your brothers were right to look out for you. Though a lot of what they've heard is true, some of it isn't.

"I may have had quite a few starlets on my arm, but I haven't had that many as lovers. I enjoyed the attention I was getting from the press. Who wouldn't? But I then realized I didn't want any commitments."

"So why start something with me?" she asked.

"Because I feel differently about you. I want to see if I can make what we have something different."

She stood, not sure how to respond. The memory of last night was still strong. The rejection had hurt her. But he'd explained and she admired him for that.

She walked over to the window, looking outside. Raucous laughter from the two teenagers in the pool broke the silence.

Eboni felt his presence directly behind her and when he wrapped his hands around her, she leaned back against the firm hardness of his chest.

She turned around, and his eyes immediately locked with hers. They continued to stare at each other, reading their heated message.

When he lowered his head and covered her lips with his, she moaned softly. She melted against him until she could feel his strength surrounding her. Tension arced through her as his erection pressed against her. He wanted her. That was clear.

His tongue eased between her lips, exploring.

Her lips left his for the briefest of moments.

"We could go to the bedroom," she purred.

"You're sure?" he asked.

"Absolutely."

He picked her up, lifting her as if she weighed nothing. She relaxed against him, enjoying the feel of his strength and power. Her fingers trailed along his arm.

When he reached her bedroom, he pushed his body against the door. It opened and he kicked it shut, without putting her down. He walked toward the bed, placing her gently on the silk covers.

His eyes adjusted to the darkness as he glanced around the room. He then found a small lamp by her bedside and turned it on.

She was glad he did. She wanted to see him naked and ready for her. Even now as she looked up at him from her position on the bed, she could see the bold evidence of his arousal. She remembered just last week, gazing in awe at his size. Now looking at him made her breathless.

He was magnificent. Every inch of his body stirred her until she felt so aroused she could not wait to feel him inside.

As he stretched his arms upward to pull the T-shirt over his head, his erection jerked forward and she reached instinctively to touch him.

Again, his penis jerked in reaction. She felt its heat and the warm blood pumping inside.

He tossed his shirt to the ground, gripping her hands, subduing the movement she was about to start.

"You're going to make me lose it even before I start."

She released him, not wanting that to happen. In time she'd have her wish. Now, this first time, she needed him to stay in control. She wanted their first time to be a long leisurely stroll and knew he wanted the same.

When he was done, he reached for her, skillfully slipping her shirt over her head, smiling when he realized she wore no bra.

"Beautiful," he said as he cupped one breast and then the other.

He lowered his head, tasting one dusky nipple before he moved to the next. While he suckled one breast, his fingers kneaded the other, causing her body to tighten then relax beneath him.

When he raised himself up, she felt a moment of emptiness until his hand caressed her lower body, and he pulled off her jeans and then her panties.

She felt vulnerable and exposed and wondered if he felt the same way.

When he reached for a pillow and placed it beneath her buttocks, she felt even more exposed, but watched as his mouth moved to the sweet wetness between her legs.

Lips kissed her silky mound, and she giggled as his touch began to tickle. But as soon as his fingers parted her and his tongue found its way to the core of her womanhood, her laughter caught in her throat—pure fire raced through her body.

Darren licked her, his tongue giving her pleasure that she could have never imagined. When his tongue touched the sensitive nub, she cried out as red-hot flames ignited every nerve. Then it happened. She felt as if she were falling. Molten pleasure washed her body with a powerful orgasm.

Her body shuddered with the intensity of her release and she screamed aloud her pleasure.

Slowly her body relaxed. When she opened her eyes, she watched as Darren retrieved a package from the back pocket of his pants, withdrew a condom and quickly rolled it onto his throbbing penis.

He pulled her to the edge of the bed, spreading her legs wide, and then he slowly entered her.

She gasped at the stab of pain and he stopped, confusion in his eyes.

"It's okay," she reassured him. "I'm all right."

He hesitated.

"Don't stop," she pleaded. "I need you."

He entered gently, slowly, as her body opened to accept his massive shaft.

Her body shuddered as inch after inch of his man-hood entered her, filling her with a joy she'd never experienced before.

"Are you okay?" he asked tenderly.

"I'm fine," she replied. She was more than fine. She ached for the promise of more to come.

And he gave her more. He moved back and forth slowly, the length of him sliding inside her, heightening every nerve in her body.

She opened her legs even wider, giving him total access. Her legs instinctively wrapped around his back, and with each stroke she felt as if she would combust. His speed increased and she joined him, her movements at first tentative until she found her own rhythm.

Darren was not a silent lover. While he stroked her, he made love to her with his words.

He whispered things that made her feel like a woman and increased the level of her excitement.

Soon, her body tensed and she could feel the first hint of her release.

She slowed her own movement, but he continued with strong, powerful strokes, until his body tensed and she knew that like her, his release was near. His thrusting became jerky, and his body began to shudder with excitement. Her own body joined his and the sweet pain of her orgasm sent her soaring. She screamed as the pleasure raced through her. Darren groaned, his body shaking, until he collapsed beside her.

She enjoyed the strength and hardness of his body close to hers. She breathed heavily, realizing that Darren's own breaths were labored.

For a while, they lay in silence. He put his arms around her, holding her closer.

Soon, his breathing steadied, and she could tell he'd fallen asleep.

The last thing she remembered thinking, before she, too, fell asleep, was that she wanted to do it again.

When Darren woke, for the briefest of moments, he was unsure of where he was. But memories of the night rushed back as quickly as the erection that now pained him. He wanted her again, but knew that she would feel discomfort.

Her virginity had surprised him. But something had happened to him in the heat of passion. He didn't want to use the word *love*. He was not ready for that, but his feelings for her had become more defined.

He shifted her arms from around him. He needed a shower.

He rose from the bed and headed for the bathroom. He flicked on the switch and a brilliant yellow light illuminated the room. For a moment, he glanced at himself in the mirror. He liked what he saw.

He'd always been lithe, but had added muscle with frequent exercise. He'd always been proud of his "tool," knowing that its length and thickness fascinated most of his conquests.

Now he looked at it in a different way. Sure, his male pride was still there, but the reality struck him. It was sad that most women found his penis more fascinating than him.

He could barely remember a time when women didn't go out with him because they wanted this part of him.

Even his wife had been the same. She'd been insatiable. Looking back, he couldn't remember when they'd even talked. He didn't know her.

With Eboni things were different. He'd felt a special yet unexpected connection. He stepped into the shower, turned the faucet on and adjusted the water to lukewarm.

He closed his eyes, loving the feel of the water on his still-heated body. He tried to keep her image from his mind, but realized he was fighting a battle he would lose.

Warm hands on his body startled him.

He turned around. Eboni stood behind him. Immediately, his body stirred, his erection coming, strong and firm.

Her hand reached down and gripped him.

"I don't advise you to do that. You'll be a bit sore from your first time."

"You pleasured me earlier. I can return the same thing."

She took body wash and lathered his erection, until he felt as if he'd spill himself in her hands, but he focused on controlling himself.

When she was satisfied she'd washed him well, she placed her mouth on him and again he fought to maintain control.

She sucked his length as it slid in and out of her mouth. There was something exciting about watching her head move back and forth, but pleasure forced him to close his eyes and all he could feel was the warmth of her mouth on him and the sweet sensation along the length of his manhood.

Soon, his legs began to weaken and his body began to shake. She replaced her mouth with her hand and as his muscles contracted and released, she stroked him. His release came in a powerful rush and he groaned out loud with the intensity.

His legs buckled and he almost fell, but Eboni held him tightly.

He opened his eyes and smiled at the look of wonder in hers.

As the water rained down on them, he searched in his memories. In all of his life, he could not remember being so satisfied.

The next time Eboni awoke, she was alone. A feeling of dread washed over her, but she remembered that Darren had told her he had an early meeting.

She stretched, embracing the feeling of contentment. The soreness between her legs was a reminder of what had happened the night before. She knew she was blushing, but in the light of day, she could not believe some of the things she had done. She'd never been much of a prude, but the things she'd said and done were very vivid images in her mind. Her arousal was evidence enough of Darren's impact on her.

What was she going to do? Though they'd become lovers—or should she say, *they'd made love?*—she still had no idea about the real nature of their relationship. Were they lovers or just friends with benefits?

She knew what she wanted them to be. She could not imagine not being in his arms and making love again. It was too early to think about anything long-term or even a happily-ever-after, but she knew she wanted him.

Memories of her sisters and their nightly ritual of storytelling came to mind. Their mother had read all the wonderful stories, but had transformed the traditional heroines into heroines of color with their own unique stories.

She smiled, remembering those wonderful times. She wondered what her sisters were doing right now. Did they remember those same times? Were they, wherever they were, thinking about her, too?

She rose from the bed. Today was going to be a wonderful day. She was falling in love with the most wonderful man.

She gasped and stopped in her tracks.

Where did that come from? Was she falling in love? Was this what falling in love felt like?

She wasn't sure. She hoped that her reaction was a result of the magnificent lovemaking.

The phone rang and drew her from her musing. She had to get a hold of herself.

She raced to the phone and picked it up before it stopped ringing.

"Eboni, it's Darren."

"Hi," she replied politely. She tried to hide the happiness she felt.

"Sorry I had to leave without saying goodbye. I did tell you that I had an important meeting but was not sure if you would remember or not."

"I remembered," she said. "Thanks for calling."

"We're actually taking a short break," he said. He paused. "I had to call you."

"You did?" Happiness surged inside.

"Yes. I've been thinking about you all morning, about us, about last night."

"Me, too," she whispered softly.

"What did you say?" he asked.

"I said, 'Me, too.'"

He laughed. "That's good to hear." He paused.

"Don't you have to get back to your meeting?" she asked, trying to change the subject.

"Okay, you're feeling all embarrassed. I'll leave the dirty talk for tonight."

"Tonight?" she asked.

"Yes, when I come over. I can come over, right?" he asked.

"Of course," she said quickly then paused. "I want to see you."

"Good. I'll be home early. Tomorrow, I'm taking you out to dinner. So you have all day to make yourself even more beautiful."

"Is there an invitation somewhere in there?" she asked.

Darren chuckled. "Oh, you want me to be a gentleman?"

"It would help, if you really want me to go out to dinner with you," she teased.

"Eboni, my beautiful next-door neighbor, lover and friend, I'd love to take you out for dinner tomorrow night. Will you honor me with your company?"

"I most definitely will," she replied in a pseudo British accent.

"Then, it's a date."

"Yes, but only if you drop by tonight," she teased.

"Oh, the young lady does want another night of passionate lovemaking. I am more than willing to oblige." He laughed. "However, while I am enjoying this stimulating conversation, I'm getting the signal from my secretary that the meeting is about to start again. Bye, my honey," he said, before disconnecting the call, but not before she heard a trail of laughter in his voice.

For a while she sat by the sofa, thinking about the significant changes in her life. There was a part of her that was scared. She wasn't even sure where all this was heading, but she was on board to give it a try. She remembered once hearing the words *it is better to love badly than to not love at all.*

The fairy tales they'd read as children had been just that—childhood fantasies.

The story had been about love, romance and happily-ever-after. Reality was a lot harsher. There was no telling the future of this relationship and while those childhood fairy tales were a part of the fantasy, they rarely happened in real life.

As a little girl, she had envisioned a life with her sisters and parents. And then tragedy had changed their lives completely.

When she'd hired the private investigator she'd wondered if she were doing the right thing.

Maybe her sisters were happy and didn't want to be reminded of the past.

But she'd had to try. If too much time had passed for there to be a joyous reunion, at least she would know that now.

She glanced up at the clock. Time for her class at the gym. She needed to have a good workout. With the stamina Darren had, she needed to be very fit to keep pace with him.

With a smile on her face, she headed to the kitchen to make breakfast.

She was going to need all the energy she could muster. The lovemaking thing did have a strange appeal.

"Stand on your toes, then stretch. Lower your shoulders and relax." Eboni paused, her eyes focused on the group of women. "That's the end of the class for today. I'll see you all next time."

There were cheers and several loud groans before the class slowly dispersed, smiles of contentment on some faces.

"So how about us girls hanging out for a bit?"

Eboni turned around and squealed. It was Cheryl, one of her colleagues from work.

"What are you doing here, girl?" Eboni asked.

"Captain Ward owed me a day off for working overtime. I know I usually come in on the weekend and late at night, but when I heard you had a class this morning, I wanted to make sure I got here. Of course, my mother-in-law decided to drop by for a *chat*. I tried to do everything I could to get her to go. It's a good thing I love her."

"I'm glad you came. How are Calvin and the boys?"

"They are fine. Calvin has been asking about you. I can't believe it's been over three weeks since I helped you move in. We've missed you at work. Want to do some shopping and then lunch after we work out?"

"Sure," Eboni replied. "In fact, I need a new dress for tomorrow."

Cheryl squealed. "You have a date! Girlfriend, I'm listening."

"Let's go work out, and I'll give you all the details at lunch."

"Can we do lunch first and then go shopping after," Cheryl pleaded. At Eboni's look of reprimand, she added. "Okay, okay, shopping, then lunch."

An hour later, Eboni and Cheryl stepped into Macy's, obvious glances thrown their way.

"We have eyes on us," Cheryl whispered.

"Eyes on us?" Eboni asked.

Cheryl tossed her hair and smiled at the man who watched as they walked by.

"We must look hot. He's gay and still staring at us."

"Cheryl, you are so crazy. How do you know he is gay?"

"Oh, I just know these things. Had a best friend in college who was gay. But come, let's get a move on. I saw the most delightful little number in here last week. I can't wait for you to try it on."

"Me?"

"Yes, you. Didn't you say you needed a dress for your 'date' tomorrow?"

"I did, but Macy's?"

"Yes, Macy's. You're rich, so you can afford to

splurge sometimes. The dress is on sale, so hopefully not all of them are gone."

Eboni realized it didn't make sense protesting. She just breathed deeply and followed.

Half an hour later, Eboni stood in front of the mirror wearing a dress that must have been created in heaven. It fit her to perfection. It hugged every curve and made her feel like a strong, sexy woman.

"Perfect," Cheryl said, echoing her thoughts. "And you don't have to look at yourself as if you didn't know you were beautiful."

She knew she was attractive, but the woman staring back at her was stunning.

"I can come over tomorrow night to help you get ready," Cheryl offered.

"I'm quite capable of getting myself ready."

"And here I was hoping to get a peek at your mysterious lover."

"In time, in time," Eboni promised. "You are too impatient."

"Okay, just want to make sure that whoever is sexing my girl is worthy."

Eboni gasped.

"Don't be shocked. You know me. I'm not one to be diplomatic."

"For sure," Eboni agreed.

"So how is he?" Cheryl prodded.

Eboni gasped again.

"Pray tell. No one is around. Just us girls."

"He was fine."

"Fine? That's all you have to say," Cheryl protested.

"He was fine. I want to know if he rocked your world, made your toes curl and made you scream for the whole building to hear."

"Yes," Eboni finally replied. "He was that and more."

"Now you're getting dirty. So is he large? I don't ever want a man with a short wee-wee. I'll buy me one of those electronic gadgets first. Fortunately, Calvin lives up to my expectations."

Eboni laughed and was about to respond, when a woman entered the changing room. "Can we leave this for over lunch?"

"Sure, hon, as long as I get all the dirty juicy details. But let's get you out of this dress. I'm so hungry I can eat two men in a Spider-Man costume."

Eboni could not help by laugh. Cheryl was outrageous, but she had a heart of gold.

When Eboni stepped out of the bathroom that night, a wave of fatigue rolled over her. She limped slowly into the bedroom, her feet still sore from her shopping trip earlier. In her bedroom, a new dress and lots of Victoria's Secret items waited to be a part of tomorrow night's transformation.

The doorbell rang and she wrapped the towel around her.

When she opened the door, Darren greeted her.

He stared at her with eyes hot with desire, the same desire reflected in her eyes.

He stepped inside and closed the door behind him. Immediately, he pulled her to him.

He took the ends of the towel and pulled them apart and watched as it fell to the ground.

"I've been thinking of you all day."

She smiled. His words echoed what she had been about to say.

"You are so damn beautiful," he continued. "I could take you right here and now."

"I think it'll take a bit too long to get to the bedroom," she agreed.

He reached for the towel on the floor, spreading it onto the carpet. He waited until she was lying on it and made short work of his clothes, tossing them aside after he pulled a condom from the pocket of his pants.

He lowered himself to the floor and settled his body between her legs. She widened her legs, giving him easier admittance.

He took the condom and rolled it on his turgid length.

"I want you now. We'll have the whole night to cuddle."

As he said this he slipped inside her, his single thrust startling her with its force, but she groaned at the powerful pleasure racing through her.

"Oh, my God, you feel so good inside me," she whispered.

"I've been dreaming of this moment all day."

"Then stop talking and make love to me."

He smiled, before he started thrusting in earnest.

Eboni awoke slowly. Light forced its way between the curtains, allowing her to see the outline of the man sleeping next to her.

She enjoyed seeing him naked. Even now he slept on his back, his legs slightly apart, and his manhood lying against his stomach.

She inhaled deeply, the image of him inside her vivid. Even now, she wanted him again and wondered if she would ever tire of wanting him.

Darren stirred, his eyes slowly opening.

"Morning, beautiful." He reached over and kissed her gently on her cheek.

"I was about to say the same thing."

"Me? Beautiful? You mean this old mug."

"Old mug? You can't be more than thirty years old. That's not old."

"Thirty-two, in fact, and I've lived a long, hard life, little princess. I've earned the right to say I'm old."

"Maybe *wise* is a better word."

"Wise? Definitely not. At least not when it comes to women."

She did not respond.

"I didn't mean you. I may be cautious about relationships, but I think you are the best thing that has happened to me in ages," he said, immediately observing the hurt in Eboni's face.

Her hurt dissipated. He did know how to say the nicest things. And he sounded genuine.

He pulled her toward him, putting his arms around her and resting her head against his chest.

"While I would love to make love to you again, I need a little more sleep. I have a busy day ahead of me."

"That's fine. This is perfect."

He mumbled something she didn't understand and in time his breathing slowed.

She didn't even realize when she joined him in dreamland.

Chapter 5

When Darren woke an hour later, Eboni was gone. A note on the dresser informed him that she had gone to teach one of her fitness classes.

He quickly put his clothes on and headed to his own place. Today was going to be a hectic one. He had several meetings and then planned on working in the office until early evening.

He was looking forward to his date with Eboni that night. He'd not been on a date in ages. Well, a real date. He had escorted a few of his lady friends to events. Inevitably, he would end up in bed at their apartments, never his. He'd make love to them and head home.

And then something struck him. He'd spent the night at Eboni's home. Twice. He'd never ever done that. Strangely enough he hadn't even realized it until now.

It hinted at the comfort level he felt around Eboni

when he wasn't thinking of the reasons not to get involved with her.

He was sure that was not an alternative anymore. They were involved. His initial discomfort at his response to her had been replaced by an ache to be with her.

Emotions were the strangest things. Even now the fact that he was thinking about her and their relationship was so out of character for him.

In the past, even with his ex-wife, the nature of the relationship had been physical. He'd genuinely liked her, and loved the sex, but upon reflection he knew they'd had nothing in common.

He wasn't even sure what he and Eboni had in common, but he had every intention of discovering what she liked and didn't like to do.

He wanted to share with her. He wanted to find out about her childhood and what had made her choose her career. He wanted to know about her family. He wanted to know her in every sense of the word.

She made him laugh and that alone said a lot. It wasn't the polite diplomatic kind of laughter. It was the loud type of laughter that came from deep inside his gut. She did that to him and it felt good.

He took a shower and got dressed quickly. About an hour later he was at his desk on the twentieth floor of his downtown office. In the distance, he could see the sign for Pace University. He'd studied at Harvard, and had disappointed his parents when he'd decided to go into real estate before taking the bar exam.

Not that they hadn't supported his choice. They had

been disappointed, yet they had not once expressed their discontent.

Unfortunately, his mother had not lived to see how successful he'd become. A drunk driver had taken her life without warning one night on her way home from the store. His father had lived longer, but two years ago lost a valiant battle with cancer. Even now he felt the familiar surge of anger whenever he thought of losing them. He'd loved his parents and missed them terribly.

The phone rang suddenly and when he picked it up, his daughter's voice came over the line.

"Hi, Daddy. It's Kenya."

"Yes, Kenya. I do recognize my daughter's voice."

"Okay, Mommy told me to call you and let you know I can't come this weekend, but I'll be there in two weeks instead of four."

He hated when his wife did this.

"Mom knows you're going to be angry, but I have a school tour this weekend in D.C. Mommy's going as one of the chaperones, so you don't need to be worried. She says she has to come into New York, so I'll be coming early." She breathed deeply. "That's it. I think I remembered everything."

"Well, enjoy you trip to D.C. You'll have to tell me all about it."

"I will. Love you, Daddy."

"Love you, too, sweetheart. Tell your mother I'll give her a call."

"Oh, that's what I forgot. She told me to tell you to call her."

He laughed. "I won't tell her you forgot."

"Okay. Bye, Dad."

As usual, he felt that emptiness whenever his daughter called. He missed her so much it hurt. Fortunately, summer was near and for four glorious weeks, he'd have Kenya with him.

He needed to tell Eboni about her, but there was time. He wasn't sure that she was ready to hear about the daughter and ex-wife he had.

What he wanted to focus on right now was getting to know her. All the other stuff would come later.

The past wasn't important.

Evening took forever to arrive. Around six o'clock, Eboni stepped out of the bathroom.

She had an hour to get ready and she wanted to make sure she had enough time to transform herself into the woman she wanted to be. She hadn't dressed up in a while but the promise of seeing the latest rage on Broadway was appealing enough. She'd been surprised when Darren had told her where they'd be going before dinner. She loved the theater but didn't associate him with that pastime.

A half hour later, she glanced in the mirror and sighed with contentment. She looked good. More than good.

She had Cheryl to thank for the dress. It was definitely perfect for her.

She grabbed her handbag and was heading to the living room when the doorbell rang.

She glanced down at her watch. He was on time.

She changed directions and headed straight to the door. When she opened it, it took all her willpower not to drag him inside and take him to her bedroom.

The Darren Grayson standing before her had been transformed into a suave, sophisticated dreamboat. Damn, he looked good.

"You clean up well," she teased. "I almost didn't recognize you."

He laughed in response, a twinkle of humor in his eyes.

"I could say the same thing about you, but you always look great. Tonight, I'm going to be the envy of every man wherever we go."

"Thanks for the compliment. All the credit goes to my friend, Cheryl."

"I must meet her and let her know she has excellent taste."

Eboni felt an unexpected twinge of jealousy.

She didn't want Darren meeting Cheryl. Men loved Cheryl's brash sexiness. She planned on keeping Darren all for herself.

"Are you are ready to go?" he asked. "Our carriage awaits us."

He followed her down the corridor and then into the lobby. Outside, a limousine awaited them.

"I was going to drive," he commented, "but since I have something special planned, I thought it would be best to have a driver."

The chauffeur opened the door for them and made sure they were comfortable and seated.

As the limo accelerated, the light inside dimmed, and the cool strains of jazz filled the interior.

Eboni was still at a loss for words. While driving in comfort like this was not new to her, her family didn't do it often, reserving the extravagance for special occasions.

Was this date a special occasion for Darren? She didn't see him as the kind of person to flaunt his wealth.

"I'm looking forward to tonight," he said, drawing her from her thoughts. "I hope you enjoy the show we're going to."

"Which show are we going to see?" she inquired, curious to know.

"You'll see when we get there. I did hear you mention it as one of the shows you'd like to see, so I made sure I called and reserved tickets. I was lucky to get them so late."

When the limo pulled up outside of the Richard Rodgers Theatre, it took all her willpower not the wrap her arms around his neck and kiss him.

She'd been trying to get Cheryl to go see *Porgy and Bess* with her for the longest time, but for some reason, their plans never worked out. The fact that he remembered she wanted to see it made her feel special. Yes, tonight was going to be a special night.

As he helped her out of the vehicle, she could not help but smile.

"I see you like my choice."

"You knew I'd love it. I've wanted to see this for ages. I love Audra McDonald, and her winning the Tony last year only made me more determined to see her in action."

"I'm glad you are pleased. Well, let's not stand outside gaping at the poster. The show will begin in about twenty minutes."

Darren turned to look at the woman seated next to him. For the duration of the first half she'd said nothing, but discussed the performances with eagerness during intermission. He'd had to force her to the concession stand. She'd not wanted to leave in case they missed something. Of course he had to promise they'd be seated way before the second half began.

Now he could not stop the occasional glance at her. Her face, rapt with her excitement and focus, revealed another side of the woman who'd completely enchanted his world.

Sitting next to her, he felt like a small child seeing his first show. He'd been to a few Broadway shows, but this one was different. Being with her made it different.

"I love this song," she whispered to him, as Audra broke into a soaring rendition of "Summertime."

He smiled, not sure what to say. Instead, he reached for her hand, squeezing it gently as he held it, to let her know that he, too, approved.

Her body tensed briefly, until enjoying the feel of his touch she slowly relaxed.

When the show ended and the curtain call took place, she stood, clapping with wild abandon, tears filling her eyes.

Outside, the limousine was waiting to take them to the restaurant for a late dinner.

Though he'd driven in Manhattan hundreds of times, tonight felt different. He felt the spirit and magic of the city.

He could tell Eboni had been affected, too. He'd felt her exuberance in the theater, but now she'd become pensive as if, like him, the music and story of the musical had deeply affected her.

"Are you okay?" he asked.

"I'm fine, just thinking about the show." Her response confirmed his suspicion.

"I haven't seen a Broadway show in years that had that kind of impact on me," she continued. "I'm always thrilled with the spectacle, but the message is still as powerful as when the Gershwins wrote it years ago."

"It was powerful," he agreed.

"You thought that, too? I was hoping you enjoyed it. I know you chose it because I said I wanted to see it."

"I'm glad I came. I've been to a few Broadway shows, but mainly plays. I don't much like musicals, but count me in whenever you want to go see a show. I'll see anything you recommend."

She turned to look at him, as if she were seeing him for the first time.

"Yes, I can be as sensitive as the next guy," he teased. "I do have my moments when I am human."

She tapped him on the arm. "I never said you weren't sensitive or human."

"It wasn't what you said, hon. It was that look," he responded. "But I do understand what you mean."

"I'm sorry. I didn't mean to offend you."

"No offence taken. I know what you mean, and you have hit it directly on the head. But no more about that. We've arrived."

When they were escorted out of the limousine, a horse and carriage was there waiting.

His eyes went straight to her face. He wanted to see her reaction. Her look of wonder was priceless and he knew he'd never forget that moment.

There was something magical and enchanting about Eboni that touched him in a way he didn't quite understand. She reached into a part of him that he had locked up for years. Unconsciously, she had dug under the hard cloak of his cynicism and touched something cold inside. He felt vulnerable and exposed, a feeling he didn't quite like, and immediately he tried to put his guard back up, but realized that for tonight, he needed it to be like this. If nothing happened between them beyond this night, he wanted to remember her this way.

"Ready for dinner?" he asked. "I'm not sure they'll keep our reservations too much longer."

Even as he spoke, she suspected that if that situation were to occur, the restaurant staff would probably bend over backward to accommodate him.

He cleared his throat, and she remembered he'd asked her a question.

"Yes, we can go in. I'm starving."

Within seconds of the hostess's greeting, they were led to a table, nestled in a dimly lit alcove, candles casting shadows that danced off the walls.

"This is really nice. I've never been here before."

"The restaurant only opened a few weeks ago. A colleague of mine suggested it. Told me he brought his wife here for their anniversary just after it opened. He said the food is phenomenal."

Eboni flipped open the menu, its sophisticated look displaying food that made her mouth water.

"Everything looks so good," she said. "But there are no prices on the menu."

"It's fine. You just need to order. When I take a woman out to dinner, I don't worry about the cost. This is one of the reasons I work my ass off. I made a decision when I was young that money would never be a problem. My father always emphasized a good work ethic to us. While he was well-off, he always said that we still had to work for what we wanted. And he made sure we did. I'm better off because of it."

"You have brothers and sisters?" she asked.

"One brother and two sisters, but they all live on the West Coast... Seattle, to be exact. Both sisters are married and living happily ever after. My brother's an up-and-coming actor, we hope. He just had his first major role, but the movie is not out until summer."

"You must remind me when it comes out. I'd love to see it. Is he any good?"

"He's definitely talented, though it took a while for him to move out of the stereotypical roles. For the first few years, all he could get were gang-member roles. He almost gave up."

"Well, I'm glad things are working out for him. I hope I get to meet him sometime."

"I'm sure you will. He comes to visit every so often.

However, I know he's working on a new movie, so I don't expect to see him for a bit."

He stopped, looking straight ahead. "The waitress is on her way. We really have to decide what we want."

Eboni glanced at the menu again. "I've decided on the smoked salmon with potatoes."

"Good choice. I'm partial to a big, juicy, well-done steak."

"I'm going to have to help you improve your diet," she commented.

"And that's coming from someone who has a sweet tooth," he interjected.

Before she could respond, the waitress came to take their orders.

For a moment, they were silent, absorbed in their thoughts.

As the waitress walked away, a strident screech broke the silence. There was a flash of bright red as a tall blonde sashayed across the room and came to a stop behind Darren.

He stood, a smile on his face, but Eboni could tell he was annoyed.

"Darren darrrling, how are you doing?" she purred in a fake British accent. "You haven't dropped by the apartment in ages." The blonde turned her face in Eboni's direction, a telling smirk on her face.

"I've been doing fine, but work has kept me pretty busy."

"Along with this *little* girl." She sniffed the air. "You could do much better than her."

"I think it's time you left. I won't have you insulting my friend." Darren's body became rigid with anger.

"If that's your wish, my dear. You know where to find me."

"Don't hold your breath, Celeste. That's not likely to happen," Darren said. "Have a good night."

After Celeste left, Eboni could see Darren was trying to control his irritation.

"I'm sorry about that," he said, concern in his eyes.

"It's okay. I have some crazy friends, too," she replied, trying to make light of the situation.

"No, it isn't. She tried to embarrass you."

"Well, I can assure you she did not succeed," she stated firmly.

"I bring you out on a date and you had to deal with that. I'm sure there are all kinds of thoughts in your head. Negative ones."

"When I came out on our date, I came knowing you had a past and a reputation. It's something I have to deal with. I made the choice to deal with it." She paused. "Yes, I'm a bit upset, but I'm not going to let it ruin our night. I've been enjoying myself. I plan on continuing to do so."

He did not reply but instead stared at her.

"You're incredible," he said. "Most women would have either walked out or insisted on being taken home. You... I don't know what to say."

"Well, you can thank God I'm still here and hurry up and order dessert. I can't wait to have some of that cheesecake."

He laughed. "Cheesecake it is. But I will make you

this promise. Those women are a part of my past. I can't guarantee that I won't encounter the occasional lady I used to know. But I don't want to be with them. I want to be with you."

Eboni nodded and reached out to place her hand on his. "I understand," she said. "Now that that's settled, can I have my dessert?"

Darren laughed again and raised his hand to signal the hostess.

The encounter with the woman from Darren's past had affected her more than she had acknowledged, but she had to trust him if she planned on having a meaningful relationship.

She had to give him the benefit of the doubt and there was no evidence that he was seeing other women. He'd made sure that tonight was for her. He'd definitely made her feel special.

Eboni placed her spoon on the plate and sighed with contentment.

"That was the best meal I've ever eaten. Every single course was delicious. I wonder where the chef trained. Had to be either France or Italy. He's just so good."

"I totally agree."

"I know I'm going to have to work out an extra hour tomorrow."

"You seem to enjoy working out."

"Oh, absolutely. I can't go two days without working out. I enjoy teaching fitness, as well. I knew I didn't want a traditional job. I got lots of flack when I decided to become a firefighter. Of course, my parents wanted me in a traditional white-collar job. I did very well in high school. In fact I was the valedictorian, the one most likely to be a doctor or lawyer. I cringe every time I think of being a doctor."

"Must have taken your parents a lot to let you go after your dream."

"Not really. I knew they were upset, probably still are, but when they realized it was truly what I wanted to do, they didn't fail to offer support. While Omar wants to be a journalist and Kemar a psychologist, the fact that they have chosen traditional careers has given Mom and Dad some comfort."

"What does your other brother do?"

"Maxwell is the math genius in the family. He's an accountant and is a partner at one of the largest firms on Wall Street. I think he loves numbers more than he loves people."

"Sounds like a young me. Originally, I wanted to be a lawyer or an accountant, but then I realized that real estate was where the money was. What does your father do?"

"Dad became the doctor and mom the lawyer. Both have done really well in their fields and have reputations of being the best. One of the reasons I must be a disappointment to them."

"Why do you keep putting yourself down? Have they ever told you that you were a disappointment? I thought you told me they finally gave their support."

"That's true, but there is a part of me that feels I've let them down. After all they've done for me."

"But it's a parent's job to do what they can for their children."

She hesitated before she spoke.

"I'm adopted."

"Oh, you are adopted and that's why you feel this way about your parents?"

"Maybe. I know they've done everything they could do for me. They've never treated me any different from the boys. In fact, I often think I get away with a lot of stuff the boys didn't. I know they love me. But there is a part of me that doesn't feel as if I completely belong. Their blood doesn't flow through my veins."

"I think I understand. So what about your biological family?" he asked.

"I have three sisters, but we were separated when I was adopted. I don't know what has happened to them. I do know, via a private investigator, that one of my sisters was never adopted, only the other two were."

"So you've been trying to find them?"

"Yes, I started looking a few years ago when I received my trust fund. I didn't want to ask my parents since I didn't want to hurt them."

"Maybe if you'd told them they would have been all right with it."

"Maybe, maybe not. I wasn't sure and didn't want to take the risk of hurting them. I've hurt them enough already."

"Don't worry. Things will work themselves out in time. Just be patient." He glanced down at his watch. "It's getting late. It's about time I took my princess home."

"I am getting a bit tired. It's been a busy day. Thanks for a truly wonderful night."

"The pleasure is all mine," he responded, the heat flaming in his eyes.

The ride back to the apartment complex was uneventful. Eboni had fallen asleep, her head rested against his shoulder.

He inhaled deeply, loving the soft fragrance of pinecones. It reminded him of the perfume his mother used to wear.

He was falling in love. He knew it. He dreaded it. But he couldn't help it.

He hoped that when they reached home, she'd invite him up. He wanted to make love to her, but even more he wanted to sleep with his arms around her, to wake up in the morning next to her.

She stirred next to him, and he felt his manhood awaken.

The limousine pulled into the parking lot and he shook her gently, watching her slowly come awake.

She smiled.

He smiled in return.

"We're home. Think you can make it?"

She giggled. "You can carry me."

"Fair enough."

He lifted her gallantly, enjoying the feel of her against him.

Upstairs, he laid her gently on her couch. She looked up at him, expectancy on her face.

"I thought you were tired," he said.

"I am," she replied.

"So why are you looking at me like that?" he asked.

"Like what?"

"Like you want to ravish me," he said.

"Oh, I do," she cooed softly.

She stood, and let her dress slip off her shoulders and down to the floor.

"And I want you to ravish me, too," she said, her voice husky with desire.

She slipped out of the tiny slip of fabric and stood before him. Damn, she was beautiful.

She hadn't turned the lights on, but beams from the full moon outside caressed her, making her even more beautiful. He could sense the magic in the air.

"Make love to me, Darren," she begged. "I want you to make love to me."

He reached for his clothes, making quick work of them until they lay on the ground next to hers in a neat mound.

He was about to reach for her, when she moved toward him. She pushed him onto the couch and straddled him.

She rubbed him, causing his penis to jerk with each movement.

He sat still, allowing her control. Inside, he felt as if he would catch on fire.

"A condom," she demanded, holding a hand out.

He bent over, reaching for his pants. He found the condom, gave it to her and watched as she rolled it over his turgid flesh. With each roll of the condom, his body jerked, the bolt of lightning racing along his body, his penis hard with excitement.

When the condom was in place, she lowered her body on his, his penis entering her slowly.

Above him she moaned.

"God, you feel so good," she groaned. "I can't even breathe."

As she spoke she moved her body over him as he lay on his back. She slid up and down, her muscles tightened around his erection, the sensation causing tightness in his body.

Her eyes were closed and she moved up and down on him. Then she opened them slowly, her eyes immediately locking with his.

They stared at each other, oblivious to everything around them.

Slowly, he joined her, his hips thrusting upward until, with each stoke, he buried himself deeper inside her.

Her breaths had deepened but her soft cries stirred him even more.

He reached up for her, placing her on all fours, and entered her warmth from behind, his penis slipping easily into her womanhood.

He stroked her firmly, enjoying the feel of his torso against her behind. He moved inside her slowly.

"Please, faster. I'm not going to break," she urged him on.

Darren consented. While he loved a slow, leisurely pace, he understood her urgency.

He stroked her deep and hard, the sound of her moans sweet and stimulating.

She was wet and soft and with each stroke he could feel the tension build inside. But more so he felt closer to her, as if there was an intricate link between the two of them.

Their bodies molded and entwined as the rhythm of the music coursed between them.

She begged him, he urged her on and then he felt it. That telltale clenching of his testicles and the surge of power. His strokes became erratic, but his lower body still moved back and forth. Then he felt the muscles of her womanhood grip him, clenching and relaxing with the same urgency he was feeling. When he thought he couldn't take the pleasure and pain anymore his body tensed with the force of his orgasm. He heard himself shout and beneath him Eboni screamed, a wondrous sound that joined his.

Slowly, his body relaxed, and he realized he was still lying on top her. He shifted slightly, hoping he was not crushing her with his weight.

"Don't move," she gasped through labored breaths. "Please don't move."

He looked down at her. She was crying.

He didn't know for what.

Had he hurt her? Had he been too rough?

"Did I hurt you?" he asked.

"I'm fine. I've never experienced anything like that before."

He lowered his head, kissing her lips gently, and when she closed her eyes, he kissed her lids.

He shifted and this time she did not object. He

reached for her and drew her close, and she settled against his chest.

As he stroked her back with his hand, her breathing slowed and soon she was fast asleep.

In the silence of the night, he whispered, knowing she would not hear.

"I love you."

Chapter 6

In the morning, Eboni awoke to the soft rays of sunlight streaming into the bedroom. Her bedside alarm clock showed a few minutes after six. She needed to get up and head to the gym. She had a spin class at seven.

Next to her, Darren moved but did not wake up.

She rose from the bed, wincing at the soreness of her body. During the night, she had awakened to find Darren watching her. They'd made love again, and then taken a shower and made love again. She was not surprised at the weariness she felt. Looking at Darren, she suspected he would be sleeping for another hour or two.

She headed to the bathroom, brushed her teeth and dressed.

Fifteen minutes later, she was at the gym, looking forward to class.

It was an all-male class of firefighters. She'd introduced the program to her captain and had been ecstatic when he had approved it. At first, the men had been reluctant, but after a few classes they were finally beginning to enjoy it.

She glanced around at the guys—a few worked with her but many were from other shifts. She remembered having a rough time when she first joined the group. But eventually, they'd accepted her. She'd thought that their initial response to her was because she was a woman.

However, she'd soon discovered that their reservations had nothing to do with her being a woman. It was about trust. Each new recruit had to play their part and earn the trust of the others. The job wasn't a solitary one. A mistake by one member of the gang could mean the death of a colleague. She'd proved herself and earned not only their trust, but also their respect. There was nothing she wouldn't do for any of them and nothing they wouldn't do for her.

She glanced around, searching for Marcus, but quickly recalled he would be missing. She still ached whenever she thought about him, still heard the screams. She blocked them out of her mind and used the remote to turn the stereo on.

By the end of the class, she felt better physically, but her body still tingled from the night of lovemaking.

Just as she said goodbye to the boys and told them she was looking forward to being back at work on Monday, her cell phone rang.

She glanced down where it lay on the floor.

It was Darren.

Her heart skipped a beat.

"Hi, Darren."

"How are you doing? I wanted to call you earlier, but remembered you had the class."

"Yes, I'm about to head into the shower…again."

He laughed.

"Do you have any plans for the weekend?" he asked.

"No, but I return to work Monday evening."

"Oh, I can have you back in lots of time."

"Have me back?" she asked.

"How'd you like to go to my home in Scarsdale?"

"Scarsdale?"

"Yes, that's where my house is. I'll talk to you about that later."

"Can I think about it?"

"Sure, that's why I called early. So you have all day to think about it. Just call me with your answer. I want to be on the road around six."

"Okay, I'll definitely let you know."

She disconnected the call.

What was she going to do? Immediately, she wanted to say yes, but caution got the best of her. She had to think about it. She'd discuss it with Cheryl—she needed another perspective before she made her decision.

She took a quick shower, dressed and walked the short distance home.

When she got in, she immediately called Cheryl.

"Hey, girl, what's your pleasure?" Cheryl's cheerful voice came across the line. Didn't her friend ever have a bad day?

"I need some advice."

"Is this we-can-talk-on-the-phone advice or should I come over after work?"

"I have to make the decision by this evening, so it's going to be talk-on-the-phone advice."

"Well, spill the beans."

"Darren wants me to spend the weekend with him at his home in Scarsdale."

"Oh, my God!" Cheryl screamed. "How romantic! Of course, you're going?"

"I haven't given him an answer yet."

"You're crazy, girl! A romantic weekend, lots of hot sex and you haven't given him an answer? Your brains are scrambled by all that good sex I assume you had on your first date—of which you've yet to give me the juicy details."

"Cheryl, it was wonderful!"

"And you had to call me to ask about this weekend? Girl, you are tripping," Cheryl chided. "You better go pack. In fact, don't pack. Just go with what you have on. You won't need any clothes. At least I wouldn't. I'd spend every minute devouring his fine ass."

"Cheryl!"

"Don't you Cheryl me. I'm sure you didn't spend last night singing lullabies to each other. So how was it?"

"How was what?" Eboni teased.

"The sex, honey. The big *O!* I hoped you screamed at the top of your lungs and had the neighbors wondering if a storm was coming."

Eboni laughed as she glanced at her watch. "Cheryl, I've got to go. I'll see you on Monday."

"Good, that means you've already decided to go. I'll

be waiting for all the hot, juicy details," Cheryl said. "I'll talk to you later."

Eboni hung up.

What had she gotten herself into?

Before she changed her mind, she picked up the phone and dialed Darren's number.

The drive to Scarsdale took a bit longer than he had expected since the traffic was heavy along I-95 to the Bronx River Parkway. But after the exit, the rest of the journey was uneventful.

Five minutes into the drive, Eboni had fallen asleep. He could see she was tired and felt guilty since he'd been partially responsible for her lack of sleep.

When he pulled into the driveway of his home, he felt the familiar surge of pride. Every time he drove up his driveway, he was amazed that this expansive property was his.

He'd been fortunate. The house had gone on sale at a time when he had the money for it. He hadn't even blinked at the three-million-dollar price tag, just wrote the check.

The attraction of the large Tudor-style house was its grandeur. He was fascinated by the architectural details, especially the oriel windows and the decorative brickwork.

When the car pulled up into the parking area next to the semicircular terrace steps, he reached over and touched Eboni gently. Immediately, she stirred.

"We're home," he said.

She looked at him strangely.

"Come on, let's go in," he told her.

By the time he exited and circled the car to open her door, she was already standing patiently outside waiting to retrieve her bag.

He frowned at her.

"I didn't see the need to wait for you to open the door for me," she said.

"Why deprive me of the opportunity to be a gentleman?" he asked.

"I assure you, there will be times I'll let you be a gentleman," she retorted. "Now isn't one of those times. I'm hungry."

He laughed. He didn't know any other woman who loved to eat like she did, and still maintained an exquisite figure.

"I gave Mrs. Clarkson, my housekeeper, the weekend off, but I am sure she left dinner for us. We'll eat as soon as we're settled."

"Good, my stomach is growling," she replied. And as if to confirm her statement, he heard a loud growl. "I did tell you so," she said with a girlish giggle.

Before he opened the trunk to retrieve their bags, he gave her the keys to the house.

"It's lovely," she said. "May I go in?"

"Sure, I'll bring the bags."

She ran up the steps to the front door, each step as buoyant as a child's. He had hoped she would like his home. Though she was the first woman he'd invited here, it felt right. Strangely enough, he hadn't even thought about whether or not to invite her to his home. But he'd given up rationalizing his actions when

it came to Eboni. Just as he'd stopped trying to ratio-
nalize his feelings for her.

He lifted their bags and followed her.

When he entered he found her racing from one part
of the hallway to another, oohing and aahing at everything she saw.

She turned around, her eyes gleaming with pleasure. "You have a lovely home," she enthused. "I've always preferred modern architecture, but I can see why
an older house would be appealing. It has…character."

"I'm glad you like it." Happiness surged through him
at her words. "You want to eat first or take a shower?"

"Can we eat first?"

"Okay. I'll put the bags upstairs and I'll be back
down." He pointed along the corridor ahead. "The kitch-
en's the first door on the right. You can't miss it. Everything should be easy to find."

He watched her briefly as she headed down the corridor before he turned to walk up the stairs. At the top
of the stairs, he heard the sound of a cell phone, but the
ring was definitely not his.

At the entrance of his bedroom, he wondered if
she'd prefer a separate room, but decided against it.
He wanted her lying next to him. He wanted to wake
up next to her.

He dropped the bags on the floor and headed quickly
downstairs.

As he walked along the hallway, he thought he heard
a strange sound coming from the kitchen. When he entered, the sight that confronted him nearly broke his
heart. Eboni was crying.

He walked to where she sat, silently, the tears flowing down her cheeks. She looked up, saw him, raced across the room and flung herself in his arms.

He allowed her to cry, relieved when her erratic breathing and tears slowly stopped.

"What's wrong?" he finally asked.

"It's the private investigator. He just called," she said through sniffles and an occasional snort.

"Bad news?"

"No, he told me he has found some information about my oldest sister. It's just a matter of time before he finds her."

"And you're crying?"

"I know. I'm happy."

"It's all right, honey." He held her tenderly, his hands stroking her head.

"Come, you can tell me all about your sisters while we eat."

He led her to one of the stools around the marble-tiled island, before he found the meal Mrs. Clarkson had left, nicely labeled, and placed the containers in the microwave. While the food heated, he poured two glasses of apple juice and placed them on the counter.

"We can eat in here, if you wish," he said.

"That's fine," she said wearily.

"You're tired?" He retrieved the containers and placed them on the counter.

She nodded.

He spooned food onto plates and carried them to where she sat. "We'll eat and then go up to bed. I'm a bit tired, too," he admitted.

She nodded again.

"Go ahead, talk. I didn't invite you for the weekend just to get you into bed." He took a sip of juice then placed the glass on the counter. "I want to spend time with you. Get to know you more." His gaze was warm as he added, "If all you want to do this weekend is relax, that's fine with me."

She looked at him, her gaze searching. "I assure you, I have no intention of spending the whole weekend relaxing."

He smiled. He liked her honesty. "I was hoping you weren't."

At his words, she picked up her fork and ate heartily. He did the same, realizing that he was hungrier than he thought. They ate in silence, and Darren could feel the sweet tension growing at her unspoken words—she wanted to make love.

When she was done, she put her fork down. "Your housekeeper is a wonderful cook," she commented. "Her food is much better than that of some restaurants I've been to."

"She's the best. I'm glad I had the good sense to keep her on when she offered her services after the former owners left. Fortunately for me, she didn't want to leave Scarsdale and start over again."

"She's definitely a find."

There was silence again, broken only by the tick tock of the clock on the wall.

"Do you want to tell me more about your sisters?"

"I have three sisters. Our parents died fourteen years

ago. I was ten and Aaliyah, my older sister, was fourteen. Cyndi was eight and Keisha was seven."

"How did your parents die?" he asked.

"In a car accident, the fault of a drunk driver. I was only ten then, but I remember being so angry."

"I know the feeling. My mother died in a hit-and-run just after I finished college. But I had my father. He only died a few years ago."

"At least you had your dad. There wasn't any other family around to take care of us."

"So what happened?" he asked

"We all ended up in a home," she paused. Telling this story was not easy for her.

"Cyndi and Keisha were adopted first and then I was," she continued. "I have no idea what happened to Aaliyah since she was still there when I left the home. We weren't allowed to maintain contact with each other. I don't know where any of them are now."

"Not knowing what happened to them must be hard." He reached out and placed a hand in hers. He wanted to offer her comfort.

"I thought it would be, but when I came to the Wynters, things just seemed so perfect. In no time, I felt that everything would be okay. I thought about my sisters all the time, and hoped that they were with good families and were happy. Especially Cyndi and Keisha."

"What prompted you to start looking for them now?" he inquired.

"It was Maxwell. He knew I wanted to know and encouraged me to find them."

"Maxwell? That's interesting."

"I know your meeting with my other brothers wasn't the best way to be introduced, but they are my brothers and I love them. From the day they met me, I've been their little sister. They'd always been good to me. I know they're overprotective, but they really do want me to be happy." She smiled at him. "But that also doesn't mean I'm going to let them control my life."

"Good for you. If you show them you can take care of yourself, they'll probably back off."

She nodded, her gaze meeting his. "I know."

"When did you hire the investigator?" Darren asked.

"Over a month ago. Just around the time I purchased the condo. I haven't told Mom and Dad anything, so Maxwell is the only one who knows. I don't want to hurt them. I know they feel I have a life with them now, but I still need to find out what happened to my sisters."

"I agree. The only way you will find some kind of resolution, at the very least, is if you know what happened to them."

"I didn't mean to burden you with this."

"You didn't," Darren replied. "Why don't you go on up to the bedroom, while I clean up the kitchen. I'll join you when I'm finished."

"I can help with the kitchen," she offered.

"Maybe tomorrow. Now, scoot!"

"Thank you," she said, leaning forward and kissing him gently on the lips. She stood and walked out of the room.

Fifteen minutes later, Darren entered his bedroom and found Eboni in bed, under the covers, fast asleep. A discarded book lay next to her.

He placed the book on the bedside table and headed to the bathroom, where he took a quick shower and brushed his teeth.

Back in the bedroom, he turned off the lights and slipped between the covers.

Instinctively, she drew closer, snuggling against him. For a while he lay there, aware of her soft presence beside him, until he eventually drifted off to sleep.

A loud scream jerked Darren awake. He glanced at the clock—it was the middle of the night. Eboni was fighting the covers, but he pulled her into his arms, warming and comforting her.

"What's wrong, honey?" He gently kissed her forehead then her temple. "Talk to me."

"I'll be fine," she said softly.

"Maybe if you talk about it," he urged.

"I saw a friend of mine die a few weeks ago."

He kissed the top of her head.

"You remember the big fire in Brooklyn." He nodded in the darkness. "Marcus, one of my crew members, was trapped under fallen debris. I was, too, but somehow I got out. As soon as someone reached him, the floor collapsed. I saw him fall into the fire. I heard his screams. I still hear them in my dreams."

"Oh, honey. I'm so sorry."

"Hold me, Darren," she whispered against his chest.

Darren felt helpless. He didn't know what to do. All he could do was what she asked. Hold her.

He knew it was going to be ridiculous, but he started to sing…an off-key version of Darius Rucker's "If I Had

Wings." He wasn't even sure if the song was appropriate for the situation. He just wanted to sing to ease her pain.

Her breathing eventually slowed, but he continued to hold her close.

He knew she wasn't ready for a relationship. There was too much going on in her life between her desire for independence, her quest to find her sisters and the death of her colleague and friend.

He wondered how she handled it all and still remained so strong and confident.

There was so much he needed to tell her but there was a part of him that was still wary of women. They always had an agenda, some scheme. With others it had been their conscious or unconscious internal motivation—all of it usually at odds with his own plans and dreams.

As if he still had dreams. He'd accomplished what he wanted in life. He had more money than he needed and a beautiful home in an affluent neighborhood.

But it all meant nothing. What he'd realized in the past few days was that he needed Eboni. That was the only way he would have true happiness.

Darren dipped pieces of bread in the egg mixture to which he'd added grated onion, sweet peppers and a few of the spices in the cupboard. He wasn't the best cook in the world, but he could hold his own with the basics.

While he was spooning the breakfast onto two plates, Eboni walked into the room.

Damn. It took all his willpower not to take her back to the bedroom and make love to her.

She'd eventually slept like a baby, exhausted by the troubled thoughts of her sisters and her fallen companion.

He'd spent most of the night thinking and staring at her, aching for her.

"Something smells good," she said. She walked over and kissed him on the cheek.

"It's my special Grayson French toast," he told her. "I hope you like French toast."

"Yes, I do," she replied, moving to sit on one of the stools at the counter.

"Good, it's my specialty."

He placed the plates on the counter. "Juice, coffee or tea?"

"I'd love some orange juice, if you have it."

"Hon, I can give you anything you want," he teased.

"That's fine," she replied, ignoring his implication. "I just want juice for now."

He smiled in response. He noticed the slight tremble of her hand as she picked her glass up. His words had affected her.

He lowered himself to the stool next to hers, startled by the energy that coursed through him when their legs touched.

"What do you want to do today?" he asked, watching as she took a generous bite of a slice of toast.

"I'm not sure," she said, shrugging. "You're the one who lives here. You must have plans."

"I did...do, but I wanted the weekend to be about you," he said.

"So what did you have planned?"

"Today, we relax. Tomorrow, horseback riding."

"Sounds good. Just what I need before I go back to work. I'll be totally relaxed by Monday."

"Are you feeling better this morning?" he asked.

She hesitated, bit into a slice of toast and nodded.

"I'm feeling much better," she said finally. "Nothing I can't handle."

"I'm sure if you can handle those brothers of yours, you can handle anything."

She laughed out loud and stopped when she realized he was staring at her.

"It's good to see you laughing," he stated. "I was worried about you. It can't be easy dealing with all the stuff you have to and your brothers, too."

"No, it's not. I'm sorry about last night. I didn't mean to cry all over you."

"It wasn't a problem. It made me feel a bit heroic," he said. "So how are we going to relax today? Read? Cuddle? Watch a movie?"

She didn't speak right away. "I just want to have you all to myself today," she said at last.

He looked at her, his gaze bright with desire as her words warmed his heart. "We could take a dip in the pool."

"You have a pool?"

"Yes, it's out back."

She smiled shyly at him. "I'd love that."

"Brings back fond memories?" he teased.

She laughed. "I was convinced you were a pervert. Dropping your pants for everyone to see."

"Not everyone. Only you."

"Just as long as you don't drop them here."

"And here I was thinking we'd be going skinny-dipping."

"What gave you that impression?" she teased.

"It's not as if we haven't seen each other naked."

"It's not the same thing," she argued.

"You just have that hang-up about nakedness. I like to be naked, to feel the wind blowing..."

"Okay, okay," she interrupted. "You don't have to get all graphic and dirty."

"Dirty? There is nothing at all dirty about nakedness," he said. "It's natural. I love being naked."

She snorted. "You would say that. It's your male pride. You know you're well-endowed, and you want everyone to see it."

"No, I don't," he stated emphatically. "I just want you to see it."

She blushed, but looked him directly in the eyes. "Are we going to go to the pool, or not?"

"Maybe I'll get you to do something bold and daring."

"Like what?" she asked.

"Well, I've never made love in this pool," he responded.

"You haven't? I would have thought with your expertise, you would have done most things...in most places."

He laughed. "You seem to be an expert on my expertise all of a sudden," he observed.

"I think I need to change the conversation. I didn't think to bring a swimsuit, but I still need to change into something appropriate. I'm going to bring along my book, too. Is it shady around the pool?"

"Of course. I'll clean up. You go get ready."

She stared at him, already feeling the heat between them. How on earth was she going to handle him? The thought of a weekend of sexual bliss was definitely more than appealing.

Eboni slammed the book down in frustration. She was getting a bit tired of this I-didn't-bring-you-here-for-sex attitude. She wanted sex. Wanted hot, sweaty, scream-out-loud sex.

What was the sense of having an empty house and a half-naked, sexy-as-hell hunk next to her when he was fast asleep in a pool chair.

She glanced across at him, her eyes immediately going to the slight bulge below his waist.

What the hell was wrong with her? She could not get enough of him. Was this what it felt like to be in love? Or was she in lust?

Of course, she lusted after him. She couldn't help it, and didn't want to help it. She knew what she felt went so much deeper, but she had to balance her feelings for him with her desire for him. He was so much more than just a sex machine to her.

She sighed and picked the book up again.

Maybe the latest Brenda Jackson novel was not the best book to read when she was as horny as a teenager. She closed the book again.

Yes, maybe a dip in the pool would be better to lower the heat. She'd told Darren to turn the pool's heater off.

Summer was coming and soon the heat would be unbearable.

But she still didn't have a swimsuit. She glanced across at Darren. He was still asleep. She could see the gentle rise and fall of his chest.

She rose from the chair, stripped off her clothes and walked to the edge of the pool. She dipped a foot to test the water to be sure the heat had been turned off. It felt cool and refreshing.

She took a step forward and plunged into the pool. For a while she treaded water, and then swam to the other side and back. Feeling invigorated, she did another lap, this time making a skillful turn that any Olympic swimmer would be proud to do.

She surfaced, only to see Darren standing at the edge of the pool, his boxer shorts nowhere in sight.

"May I join you?" he shouted and without waiting for an answer dived into the pool.

For several seconds, he disappeared, but then she noticed his blurry shadow swimming toward her.

Just before he reached her, he surfaced, but not before, she was sure, he got a good look at her nakedness beneath the water.

He grinned, his face showing his delight.

"Pervert!" she said.

"Me?" he said, a broad grin on his face. "I'm not the one who was in the pool swimming naked."

"It's your fault," she spluttered.

"My fault?" he asked, treading water until he floated before her. Their bodies touched and she felt the familiar, but unexpected surge of heat. Wasn't water supposed to cool her body?

"You fell asleep and I was bored. I am supposed to be your guest," she insisted.

"I'm sorry," he said. "I must have been more tired than I thought."

"It's fine," she assured him. "I've had my swim. I'm going to go up and take a shower."

"Want some company?" he asked, his voice low and seductive.

"No, thank you. I'm feeling a bit tired. Maybe I'll get some rest."

"I'll take a few laps then come and join you. I'm a bit tired, too." He grinned again. "I don't want to leave you on your own too much. After all, you are my guest."

She chuckled. "Throwing my words back at me?"

He did not respond. She looked at him. His grin had faded and he was silent, brooding.

He leaned forward and kissed her on the lips. The kiss lit a flame that coursed straight to her womanhood.

"I want you," he whispered. "I won't be long."

Her heart pounding, she plunged into the water and swam slowly to the edge of the pool. She got out and walked directly toward the door, only realizing as she got near the edge that she was still naked.

She stopped briefly to turn around, but decided against it. She didn't need the clothes anyway.

Chapter 7

Later that afternoon, and after a dinner of chicken Florentine with fettuccine and chopped spinach, Darren retired to his den to make a few important calls. Eboni accepted his apology and, with a smile, raced off, he assumed, to finish reading her book.

He shook his head, closing his office door behind him.

After rushing through his calls, he ran upstairs, but skidded to a stop as he reached the bedroom. His total focus was on Eboni. He was going to make her scream with ecstasy. All. Night. Long.

Soft candlelight filled the room, the shadows and light dancing like lovers in the corners. Eboni lay on the bed, the warm glow caressing her scarlet lace lingerie even as it beckoned him to seduction.

His erection was immediate, forcing a groan from

between his clenched teeth. What had she done to the room? He decided he didn't care when or how—he just knew he was about to have one of the best nights of his life.

"Come here, lover boy," she said, her voice husky with desire.

She parted her legs slowly, tempting him with a glimpse of her...but she wasn't wearing any panties. And she called *him* a pervert. He smiled.

To say he was surprised was an understatement, but he loved that about her. She wasn't afraid to be daring and bold.

His body shuddered with his excitement. He could already feel himself deep inside her and the image made his penis rock-hard.

He stood over her, his arousal reflected in her own eyes. He took his jeans off and dropped them to the floor, before sheathing and then lowering himself between her legs.

"Now," she coaxed. "I want you now."

He entered her with a single firm stroke and she gasped with its impact.

When he was buried deep inside her, he paused, his eyes locked with hers. There was no need for words. It amazed him that they were so in tune with each other.

"What are you waiting for?" she challenged. "You plan on staying there all night?"

He chuckled. "I love a woman with spunk. Hope you are up to the challenge."

She laughed in response, her inner muscles gripping his penis playfully.

With that, he moved his hips backward and thrust forward, watching her eyes close with the pleasure of his movement.

"Damn," she cried. "That feels so damn good. I don't think I'll ever have enough of you."

Urged on by her words, he stroked her again, hard and fast, increasing his momentum with each stroke.

Beneath him, she played her part, wrapping her legs around his waist, drawing him deeper inside her with each thrust of his hips.

She gripped his back, urging him on, faster, harder, as her nails scored his skin, branding him as hers—and it drove him wild.

Darren slipped a hand between them, one finger pressed against the nub at the core of her womanhood, the friction created by the movement of his penis in and out of her increasing her excitement. He felt her body contract and her orgasm came sudden and hard. He continued to stroke her, unable to control the harsh groan that escaped his lips. But he wasn't ready for his own release. He didn't want this ride to end too soon.

He kissed her, capturing her tongue and sucking on it until she moaned her pleasure. Time stopped. Only the synchronized, sensual dance of their bodies mattered.

The harsh sound of their heavy breathing, broken only by a low groan or a sharp cry of pleasure, filled the room.

And then he felt her fingers dig into his back and her body tensed again. His own body trembled in response.

He increased his speed, stroking her harder and faster. Inside, the pressure built, his rhythm faltered…

and then it happened, a glorious, joyous feeling like none he'd ever experienced rushed over him. In that moment, he felt vulnerable, as if he had taken a jump off a high cliff, but there was no sense of fear, only a buoyant feeling as he floated to the ground.

Slowly, he rolled off of her, not realizing he had collapsed on her. Next to him, her breathing slowed as his did.

He moved his hand, searching for hers, and held it as he stared up at the ceiling.

Making love to Eboni was an incredible experience. He could not understand why making love to her was so different. Each time he marveled at their coupling, and each time he was amazed by the connection that held him to her.

He moved his body, turning on his side to look at her.

She stared at him, wide-eyed and innocent, despite their making the most sinful love for the past hour.

He kissed her lips.

She blushed.

"I love making love to you," he said softly.

"You do?" she asked. He could hear the uncertainty in her voice.

"Yes, I do. Why would you think otherwise?"

"You. Your experience. I was a virgin," she said with a sense of conviction as if her comment would lessen his enjoyment.

He moved closer to her, wrapping his arms around her, their eyes and lips close together.

"You are one incredible woman. Making love to you feels different, feels right," he reassured her.

She blushed again, but the concern on her face slowly dissipated.

"I enjoy making love to you, too," she admitted. "I have nothing to compare it with, but I can't think of it being any better."

"Oh, I promise you I will make it better," he vowed.

He definitely planned on taking their lovemaking to another level each time. He wanted to please her, to make her feel good, and for her to be comfortable with their sexuality.

He kissed the tip of her nose.

"Get some sleep. You must be tired. I am."

She snuggled closer to him, resting her head upon his chest, a hand against his stomach.

His penis stirred and he groaned.

He couldn't believe he wanted her again. Would he ever get enough of her? It didn't seem like it.

She was like an obsession and for the first time in his life, he wasn't sure what to do.

He closed his eyes and slowly drifted off to sleep.

On Sunday morning, he woke to the sound of music piping through the speakers in the bedroom. The music wasn't loud, but he recognized the soothing tenor of Anthony Evans, one of his favorite gospel artists.

He jumped out of bed, wondering where Eboni was. He brushed his teeth, took a quick shower and headed downstairs. The delicious aroma of bacon and eggs teased his nostrils and when his stomach growled, he hurried into the kitchen. He was hungry.

When he stepped into the kitchen, Eboni was absorbed in the task at hand. She seemed to have found everything she needed and was singing along with the music.

She turned, gasped and almost dropped the bowl she was carrying.

"Are you trying to scare me to death?" she reprimanded.

He walked over and kissed her softly on the lips.

"Sorry, I tried to speak to you but the music was too loud."

"Oh, I'm sorry. Was I singing too loud?"

"Not really, but I would advise you not to give up your day job," he replied jokingly.

"Oh, dear, and here I was planning to try out for *American Idol* later this year."

"Oh, well, as my mother once said, you can only succeed if you try and try again."

She laughed in response.

"Breakfast will soon be done. I hope you like eggs and bacon. There are also a few pancakes and fruit salad. Juice, coffee or tea?"

"Since I can already smell the coffee, that's my pleasure. I got that coffee all the way from Jamaica when I was on vacation. A friend of mine brings it to me whenever he visits New York."

"I've been trying to cut down on the amount of coffee I drink, but without success."

"Then we're going to be no help to each other. I must have my cup to start the day. Having the rich Blue Mountain Coffee doesn't help."

"You can have a seat. Everything is already on the

table. I'll just add some bread to the toaster. Two slices or four?"

"Four," he said with no hint of shame. "I'm a growing boy and need sustenance."

"With the way you eat, I'm surprised you're so trim."

"I work out, too, but I use the gym in my office."

"Do you like your work?" she asked, lowering herself to one of the stools.

He hesitated for the briefest of moments.

"Yes, love it. But I do have a confession to make," he said cautiously.

"What is it?"

"I own the apartment building where we live."

She paused then asked, "You do?" He could hear the surprise in her voice.

"I do. I did plan on telling you before, but the right time never came up."

"You could have told me that from the first day," she snapped.

"I didn't know you then. I don't tell everyone and anyone who I am."

"Maybe when we became lovers would have been a good time."

"You're right and I'm sorry. I could have told you then. I didn't think it was that important. You know I'm in real estate."

He could tell she was upset. She remained silent for a bit as if she were trying to absorb what he had told her.

"I'm sorry. I am really being overly sensitive about this. There is no way we can know everything about each other. We're just lovers, no commitment—"

"I was thinking about that," he injected.

She nodded.

"So what do you think about us dating?" he asked.

She thought for a bit. "You mean exclusively. Commitment."

"I'm game if you are."

"Can I think about it?"

Her question surprised him, but he nodded, trying to curb his disappointment.

"You can have all the time you want. I'm not going anywhere," he said.

She nodded again. Her focus was on the plate in front of her. She spooned the last bit of food into her mouth and then set her fork down.

"Are we still going riding?" she asked.

"Can you ride? A horse, I mean?"

"Yes, my dad made sure we all learned how to ride when we were younger. Kemar almost scared Dad once when he said he wanted to be a jockey, but a year later it was something else. I'm surprised he finally made up his mind. He has one more year to go before he finishes his master's degree."

"I have a few horses at a stable nearby. I try to ride every weekend when I come home. Today's a perfect day for riding. There are several trails on the property and an area for those who want to do some jumping. I think there's also a cross-county trail if you're interested. We could take one of the trails and stop for a picnic. There are picnic tables dispersed across the property."

"Sounds like fun," she replied.

"I'll prepare the picnic basket since you made breakfast. I'll be up in a bit."

"You're sure you don't want me to help?"

"No, you go read your book," he insisted.

"Will do," she replied, turning to walk out of the room.

Darren turned to the task before him as she left.

He had been surprised that she had been so upset about his omission. Then something crossed his mind. He still hadn't told Eboni about his ex-wife and daughter. He'd make sure he did it before they returned to New York. He didn't want this situation to arise again.

Half an hour later, a well-stocked picnic basket ready, he climbed up the stairs and headed toward his bedroom.

When he pushed the door, Eboni sat on the window seat, her head buried in her book.

She looked up when she saw him and jumped up immediately.

"I'm ready," she said. She had changed into a pair of jeans and a white blouse that hugged her breasts a bit too much.

"Good, the picnic basket is ready. I just need to get into something a bit more appropriate."

He changed quickly into a pair of jeans and a Calvin Klein polo shirt.

When he looked up from lacing his boots, she was staring at him.

"What?" he asked.

"You look very handsome."

He snorted. "Thank you, hon. Are you ready?" he asked.

"I'm ready."

She followed him down the stairs, where he retrieved the basket, and then they headed out the door to the car.

Ten minutes later they were coasting along Post Road. He pointed out several landmarks of the area's colonial past. The Wayside Cottage in particular had always fascinated him.

He slowed down as they passed the cottage, drawing her interest.

"When I first moved here, I fell in love with this cottage. The earliest part of the house was actually built about 1720 and sits on a fieldstone foundation. I love the gable roof and veranda with Doric-order piers. I believe that another section of the house was built in the 1820s and the final section, known as the caretaker's quarters, was built in the late nineteenth century."

"It's all so…fascinating. Next time I'd love to see inside. Who owns it?" she asked.

"Since 1919, it has been owned by the Junior League of Central Westchester, but I am sure I can arrange it. I know the committee provides guided educational tours in period dress for local schools and community groups, but I make a healthy contribution each year to the league."

"That's good." She looked at him as if she were seeing him through different eyes.

"Why are you looking at me so strangely? I do have a good heart and believe in using my money to help a good cause. I have more than I need."

"I'm pretty impressed," Eboni stated. "I love what I've seen of Scarsdale. It's quiet and quaint. It's hard to believe that Manhattan is just an hour away. I hope it remains like this."

"With the cost of real estate here," he reasoned, "it's not going to change much. However, we've arrived at my friends' place."

He turned onto a rugged road that led to what looked like an old farmhouse.

"This used to be a farm until my friends Grant and Donna converted it into a stable. They board horses, but also give riding lessons."

When the car pulled up in the parking area, a tall, handsome man walked toward the vehicle.

"Darren, it's good to see you. Couldn't understand why you haven't been home for the past month or two. Donna told me there must be some lady keeping you in the city. She was right, I see."

"This is Eboni, a friend of mine. I invited her to spend the weekend. Eboni, this is Grant. He and his wife, Donna, own the stables."

Eboni shook Grant's hand, while Grant smiled and said, "Interesting. Must be serious. You don't usually bring—"

"Grant," he growled, "she is standing right next to us as you discuss my personal life."

"Oops. I'm sorry." Grant chuckled. "It's just my excitement to meet her. I'm sure Donna will be as excited as I am."

"I am sure. However, I am here to take the horses out."

"Which ones? She can ride?" he said, turning to look at Eboni.

"Rafe and Lady," Darren replied.

"You're sure about Lady?" Grant queried, looking a bit skeptical. "She is a bit spirited."

"I can do spirited," Eboni asserted. "I promise you."

"I'll take your word for it, but I'm sure Darren can take care of any problems," Grant reasoned.

"I assure you," she injected, a bit offended, "there won't be any problems."

"Well, Darren, you have a handful with her. She does look like she can take care of herself."

"She can. She's a firefighter."

"A firefighter!" he exclaimed. "Now, this is all very interesting." He turned in the direction of a loud shout.

A woman, dressed in riding habit, strode across the yard.

"Darren, I can't believe it's you," Donna squealed. She stopped when she reached them and planted a huge kiss on his cheek.

Then she turned to Eboni.

"And who is the beautiful young lady?" she inquired, a gleam in her eyes.

"I'm Eboni," she said, before Darren could respond.

"And I'm Donna," she replied. She reached for Eboni's hand and squeezed it tightly. "It's a pleasure to finally meet one of Darren's friends."

"I've been enjoying Scarsdale. It's a lovely place. I don't miss the noise of the city at all."

"Oh, I know you'll love it here. Darren needs someone to share that big old house with."

"Donna," Grant warned.

"You know me, Grant," she stated, pointing her finger at him. "I speak my mind. She must be special for him to bring her here. For all the years we've known him, he's never brought a friend here." She turned to Eboni. "No need to blush, sweetheart. I like you."

"Grant," Darren said, "we want to go riding. You want to go get the two horses ready."

"And what's that in your hand, Darren?" Donna said, peering at his hands. "A picnic basket? How romantic!" She clapped her hands in glee. "You must take Eboni along the northern trail and show her the pond. There's a picnic area at the end of that trail. She will love it." Donna glanced down at her watch.

"It was nice to meet you, sweetheart." She moved closer and whispered in Eboni's ear, something Darren didn't hear, but Eboni's blush suggested it was about him.

A few minutes after Donna disappeared, a groom arrived with their horses.

Darren took the reins from the groom and turned to Eboni. Before he could speak, she moved cautiously toward the horses.

"Oh, Darren. They are beautiful. I'm in love already. And Lady...she is a lady. Even if she's feisty."

She placed her hand on the white roan.

"May we go? I can't wait to ride her."

Darren waited until she had mounted before he secured the basket and mounted the black Arabian. He had paid top dollar for both horses and compensated Grant handsomely to make sure they were well cared for.

* * *

They followed the trail in silence, only pausing when Eboni wanted to take a closer look at something that struck her fancy. Each time she stopped she could feel his gaze on her, but she did not let his attention deter her. Living in New York, she rarely got the opportunity to experience nature, except for the occasional visit to Central Park.

Eboni inhaled deeply, savoring the freshness of the air. Beneath her, Lady maintained a steady canter, but she could tell the mare preferred to run with the wind. Hopefully, if she were invited to Scarsdale again, she'd have the opportunity to take the horse on a gallop.

Soon, they pulled into a clearing, the honey locust and ash trees giving way to a smattering of picnic tables in a well-maintained picnic area. The area had been skillfully created to blend into the natural foliage. Beyond the tables, ducks played in a shallow pond.

Eboni turned to Darren. "This is beautiful," she said.

"I knew you'd like it," he replied, dismounting and tethering his horse to the tie rail. Eboni followed suit as she tied Lady next to Rafe. She reached for the basket but he shooed her away.

"I'll take it," he insisted. "It's heavy."

She glared at him, walking over to one of the tables under the canopy of a vibrant honey locust tree. He followed and set down the basket.

"I'll put the food out, but for now I just want a bottle of water. Want one?" he asked.

"Sure," she replied, still annoyed at him. Why did men think that all women were weak imbeciles?

He handed her the bottle of water.

"Thanks," she said, taking it from him. Their fingers touched and he held her hand in his. Flames sparked between them.

"The water," she said, gasping for air.

He reached for her, pulling her up against him, his body pressed hard against her, his erection evident.

Her heart beat faster. She was as aroused as he was. The blood in her head pounded until she felt as if she would faint with her need for him. She now understood the meaning of the word *swoon*.

He leaned in, cupped her face and laid his mouth on hers, nibbling softly.

She closed her eyes, a warm sensation spreading through her body.

Instinctively, her lips parted, allowing his tongue to slip inside. She kissed him back, deepening the kiss, until she could taste him. His breath came faster as his hands cupped her breasts, his thumbs rubbing through the fabric to tease her aching nipples. She moaned with pleasure when he parted her legs, but immediately pulled away at the sound of laughter in the distance.

"This is definitely not the right place for this," Darren gasped.

"It appears it's not," she said, trying to control her breathing while straightening her blouse at the same time.

She sat at the table, watching as he opened the basket, his face expressionless as if nothing had happened.

Four horses appeared carrying a man, a woman and two boys.

He gave her a sidelong glance. "We'll continue this later," he promised.

She smiled. She could wait a few hours, but she anticipated what would come.

Darren lay on the bed, wondering if her shower would ever end. As soon as they entered the bedroom, he'd torn off his clothes, but after a long day outdoors, Eboni had insisted they shower. All day he'd ached for her, all day he'd wanted her, but the family's presence had made it impossible.

He'd enjoyed the company of the others at the picnic spot, like she had, but throughout the day he'd seen her looking at him with fire burning in her eyes. Just after two o'clock, after a game of football with the boys, they all decided to pack up and call it a day. The ride back to the stable and the drive home had seemed to take forever.

He heard the shower stop and his penis jerked in response. He wanted her so badly.

When she stepped into the bedroom, she'd wrapped a towel around her.

"Take the towel off," he ordered.

Immediately, she dropped it and he sucked in his breath.

She stood there, not moving, as if waiting for his next command. She thought he was in charge. Little did she know, he'd never been in charge. From the moment he'd met her, all his attempts at control had gone out the window.

"Come," he growled with desire.

She obeyed, moving seductively toward him. When she reached him, she straddled him, but he flipped her over on her back, immediately lifting her hips to bury his face in the mound between her legs.

She smelled good, a combination of woman and the floral-scented shower gel she used.

He placed his mouth against her, letting his tongue slip between the delicate folds. He tasted her. His tongue found her sensitive nub and flicked it, causing her to writhe beneath him. Her hands grabbed his head, forcing his tongue deeper inside her, until she exploded without warning, her orgasm coming powerful and strong. Her body convulsed and she cried out his name.

Darren lowered her hips, used his knees to ease her legs apart. He reached across to the bedside table, groping around until he found one of the condoms. He opened the package quickly, rolling it onto his hardened length.

He raised her legs, her wantonness exciting him even more. When he entered her, he felt as if he were coming home, as if he'd been away too long from this special place.

Her gasp of excitement echoed his. He paused for a moment, enjoying the feel of her wetness, her readiness. He rotated his hips, allowing his penis to explore all of her, the friction intensifying his enjoyment, heightening his pleasure.

And then he gave in to his body's needs. He pulled out slowly and then pressed in again…out and in, settling into a smooth rhythm.

His hands curved around her buttocks, allowing him

to thrust slowly and deep. Beneath him, she groaned, intensifying the sensation building inside him.

She clutched his back and her fingers caressed him, sending additional sensations down his back. Her teeth found his earlobe. She nipped and blew gently into his ear, causing him to shiver with desire.

He shifted his head, getting relief from the tickling sensation, and he rained soft kisses across her cheek, and then captured her mouth with his.

He watched her face, seeing the desire there. He pulled out of her slowly, and then eased in again until she begged him not to stop.

And then she groaned, a guttural sound that increased his excitement. His thrusts deepened as he moved faster in and out of her.

Sweet pain coursed along his length and he knew he was about to explode.

Her hands gripped his bottom, forcing him even deeper as she screamed her release. Her muscles clenched around him as he gave in to his own orgasm. The sweet rush of liquid along his length coaxed his own cry of pleasure as his body shook with the intensity of the energy flowing through him.

His mouth covered hers, capturing her scream as their bodies locked and rocked in the throes of ecstasy.

With their bodies still heaving, he reached for her, kissing one breast and then the other tenderly.

"Another shower and then we have to get ready to leave."

As he said the words, a sense of dread washed over

him. He didn't want to go back to Manhattan, but it was inevitable.

He had a company to run and she would be back saving lives.

Their idyllic weekend had come to an end. Tomorrow they would return to the reality of their everyday lives.

But now, he'd prolong the fantasy for a bit longer.

He rose from the bed and lifted her.

"Come take a shower with me," he insisted, pressing his erection against her.

"Only a shower?" she asked coyly.

"Come and see," he teased.

She laughed, a joyous sweet sound that filled the room with happiness.

Chapter 8

Ebony stared straight ahead at the clock on the wall as she listened to Dr. Belle's monotonous voice drone on and on. She wanted to get back to work, but she had to endure this session to make it possible.

She stifled a yawn and forced herself to focus.

"It seems to me that you are dealing pretty well with the situation. I would usually recommend another week or two at home, but I believe you're ready to return to work. However, I want your promise that if the pressure of the job becomes too much, you'll call me immediately. You know the importance of being mentally as well as physically fit."

"I know and I promise," she replied. "I don't want to be responsible for any of my colleagues' deaths."

She cringed inwardly. Was that how she felt? That she was responsible for Marcus's death? Her hands trembled. She stood abruptly and picked up her handbag.

"When is my next appointment?" she asked.

"In two weeks," Dr. Belle replied. "The usual time."

"I'll be here at nine o'clock," Eboni said. "I'll see you then." She turned and headed for the door.

"And, Eboni," Dr. Belle added, "take care."

"Thank you," she replied, then opened the door and left.

Once in the hallway, Eboni leaned against the cool wall, unable to control the trembling. She closed her eyes and breathed in deeply, then exhaled slowly. Soon the turbulent feelings subsided and she walked briskly to the firehouse.

When she stepped inside, she almost jumped out of her skin. All of her coworkers stood before the table with the largest bouquet of flowers she'd ever seen.

She couldn't speak as tears filled her eyes then ran down her cheeks.

"Welcome back, Wynter," Captain Ward said, his hand outstretched. "We're glad to have you back. The firehouse has not been the same without you."

"Thank you, sir," she replied, reaching to shake his hand.

Instead, he pulled her to him and hugged her tightly. When she stepped back, she was sure the surprise was still on her face. Captain Ward was not one for outward displays of affection.

"Well, enjoy the little get-together," he said gruffly, looking slightly embarrassed. "Hopefully, your first day back will be a quiet one."

Before he could turn and walk away, the alarm sounded.

There went all hope of a quiet day.

Immediately the chatting halted and everyone sprang into action.

The rest of the week passed in a haze of smoke and fire. Each day of her four-day week, she and the rest of the crew fought fire after fire.

By Friday night, she was cranky and all she wanted to do was soak in a tub of warm water filled with her favorite bubble bath.

When she walked into her condo that night, she could still taste and smell the acrid smoke.

She collapsed on the couch, sighing with relief as her bones melted into the cushions.

Every muscle in her body ached but she was too tired to make it into the bathroom for a long soak in the tub.

There was a knock on the door and she groaned. She hoped it wasn't her brothers. She'd kill them. She'd warned them not to come by without calling and more recently they'd taken heed to her words.

She got to her feet and dragged herself to the door. She looked through the peephole.

It was Darren.

She opened the door and stepped back to let him in. He was a sight for sore eyes.

"I hope it's okay to drop by."

"I'm glad you did."

"I missed you," he said unexpectedly. He had a sweet way of surprising her.

"Me, too."

He reached for her but she pulled back.

"Sorry, but I was at a fire all day and you don't want to hug me before I have my bath. Give me a few and I'll be back for all the hugs you want to give me."

He smiled sweetly. "How about I take a bath with you?"

"Don't be silly, I'm too filthy from work today. You can wait until I'm done. Make yourself at home."

Despite her words, he followed her, but when they reached her bedroom, he said, "I'll wait out here for you. You go take your bath. Take all the time you need."

She nodded and headed to the bathroom, forcing herself not to look back.

While she could not take the long bath she'd planned, a long shower would have to suffice. She needed to wash all traces of the fire and smoke away.

Half an hour later, feeling relaxed, her hair light and bouncy after a shampoo and conditioning, she returned to the bedroom, only to find Darren naked and fast asleep.

The sight of him stirred her. He must have been as tired as she was.

She lowered herself to the bed, moving close to him, and closed her eyes, a smile on her face.

When Darren awoke, his gaze immediately focused on the woman he loved deeply. In her sleep, she was as beautiful as she was when she was awake. He reached out to touch her, but stopped. He didn't want to wake her. She had to be tired.

He was tired, too. Work had been hectic. But he'd ended the day on a good note. He'd sold a property for close to four million. But the overwhelming sense of accomplishment he usually felt was missing. Being with Eboni made him more aware of the truly important things in life. Being with her was changing him.

With her, he felt whole and wanted. He knew that she loved their lovemaking. Sex between them was incredible, but there was something different. He never felt that sex was all she wanted. Being with her in Scarsdale had made him realize that much.

She genuinely liked him and while they were lovers, he hoped she'd eventually want more.

Even though the majority of his friends were either single or divorced, he refused to believe relationships did not work. Several of his close friends were still basking in marital bliss.

Beside him, Eboni stirred.

He willed her to wake up and when her eyes fluttered open, he smiled.

"What are you smiling about?" she asked, her voice husky with sleep.

"Nothing, really," he replied.

"Don't give me that," she countered. "I know exactly what you're thinking."

"And pray tell me what that is?" His finger trailed along her cheek.

"That you want me to make love to you."

"I do?" he said coyly.

When she didn't respond, he pulled her to him. He gripped her bottom, kneading its firmness. She collapsed against him, her body pressed into his until he could feel every toned muscle.

Her body was one of the things he loved about her. She wasn't fragile and helpless; instead she radiated strength and control. During lovemaking he never felt as if he needed to be careful.

Tonight, her hair was spread out on the pillow. He looked into her eyes, noticing the emotion there. While he knew her eyes were brown, he'd never noticed the whiskey-colored flecks in them that made them even more beautiful.

He lowered his head, plundering her mouth with his. She shivered. He could already feel the heat of her arousal, of her desire.

She broke the kiss. "I want you to make love to me, Darren." She moaned her desire, her fingers already finding his chest as she took a hard nub between her nimble fingers.

He moaned. She'd just found one of the most sensitive spots on his body.

She lowered her head and took one pebble-hard nipple between her teeth, nibbling and tugging on it until he could barely stand the pleasure.

She raised her head and looked down at him. He felt vulnerable beneath her. She had all the control.

Her mouth moved downward and she rained kisses on his chest. Stopping, she teased his navel with her tongue, the sensation making him shiver.

When her mouth reached below, she snuggled there for a moment before moving farther down. By now his erection was hard and painful and he knew that only his release would ease the discomfort.

She lovingly gripped his penis in her hand.

When her lips covered his hardness, he groaned deeply, never wanting the feeling to end. He willingly gave in to the sweet pleasure of her mouth.

Knock, knock.

Eboni groaned. Who on earth could be at her door so early on a Sunday morning?

It was probably Cheryl. But she was sure she'd told her that she wouldn't be able to go to the gym since she'd just worked a four-day shift. She hoped Cheryl hadn't just invited herself over.

She rose quickly from the bed, put her robe on and headed toward the door.

She peered through the keyhole and wanted to scream.

What the hell were all her brothers doing there so early in the morning—and uninvited? It was just after nine o'clock. Unless she was going to work, she didn't emerge from the confines of her bed until she felt like moving. She would usually watch television, read a book, sleep some more, but rarely did she get up before midday.

She opened the door angrily.

"Morning, sis," Kemar said cheerfully.

"What are you doing here?" she asked abruptly.

"Mom was worried. She hasn't heard from you in a while. We promised to stop by," Maxwell said.

She sighed. Hopefully, Darren would remain in the bedroom until they left.

So much for that.

A low, strangled sound came from Omar and she didn't have to turn around to know that Darren stood behind her. When she did turn to look at him, at least he was in his boxers.

She glanced down, wondering if, for her sake, the floor would open up and swallow her.

No such luck.

"What's he doing here?" Kemar demanded coldly.

"With no clothes on?" Omar managed to ask, finally getting his voice back.

"Sure you want to hear, boys?" Darren asked in a cool voice. Her brothers and their noticeable anger obviously had no effect on him.

"Stop," she shouted, before her brothers could get a word in edgewise.

She turned to Darren. "I don't wish to be rude, but I think it's time you go. I need to have a good talk with my brothers."

Darren smiled, walked over to her, kissed her on the lips and whispered in her ear, "You're sure you don't want me to stay?"

She smiled back at him and, loud enough for her brothers to hear, said, "I'll be okay. I need to deal with them on my own."

He nodded in understanding. "You'll do fine," he said quietly, but also not out of earshot of her brothers. "I'll be back for the rest of my clothes later."

With that statement, Darren opened the door and

heard one of her brothers snort. He turned around, his gaze narrowed on the brothers.

"I think the three of you need to take a good look at yourselves. Yeah, I understand you want to protect your little sister, but you need to realize that she isn't a little girl anymore. She's a woman. Don't alienate yourself from her with your heavy-handed behavior."

He smiled and stepped into the hallway. It was testament to Darren's control that he closed the door quietly behind him.

In the wake of Darren's departure, the room was quiet. Eboni could have cut the tension with a knife.

"He's right," she said. "And he's said all that I wanted to say. I really don't want to talk to any of you right now so I think it's best you leave. I want to talk to all of you, Mom and Dad included. I have to put an end to this nonsense."

She walked over to the door, opened it and stood aside so they could leave.

Not one of them said a word and as the last one walked out, she closed the door behind them.

She listened for their retreating footsteps. It was a full two minutes before she heard the sound.

When she was sure they were gone, she rested her back against the door, slowly slid to the floor and cried.

All cried out, Eboni finally got in the tub and had a long, hot bath, after which, she climbed into bed and fell into a deep sleep. When she awoke it was after eleven o'clock. At least she had the strength to leave her bed this time.

She had to work the next day, but she didn't want to sleep alone. She dressed in a pair of jeans and a T-shirt and headed for Darren's condo.

Ironically, she'd never been there before. They had spent most of their time together at her place.

She walked briskly to his entrance and pressed the doorbell.

She heard some rummaging and then a loud curse. She almost laughed. She hoped he'd not hurt himself.

The door opened and he stood there, a towel around his waist.

"Sorry for disturbing you."

He stepped back, inviting her in.

When he closed the door behind her, he reached for her, pulling her against him.

"Are you okay?" he asked. "I wanted to call, but I wasn't sure what happened after I left. Next time, I'm staying there with you."

"I promise you, there won't be a next time," she stated. "I'm going over to my parents' home one evening after work. I've told them all to be there. Maxwell is the only one who no longer lives there, but he had better be there."

"That's my girl. You tell them like it is. Want any moral support?" he asked.

"I wouldn't mind, but I need to do this on my own," she explained. "They have to see me for who I am."

"Okay, I know exactly what you mean," he replied. "I was as pissed as you were earlier."

"I could tell, but you're the first of my...friends to stand up to them."

"Hon, I don't exactly scare easily," he stated firmly.

"I can see that."

"No matter what happens, I'll stand by you."

She smiled, snuggling closer to him.

"So what are your plans for tonight? Want to sleep over?" he asked, a finger trailing along her arm.

"I was hoping you'd ask," she admitted. "I've grown accustomed to not sleeping alone. I'll get the grand tour tomorrow morning since this is the first time I've invited myself here. But I can already see compared to this, mine is definitely humble."

"I'm sorry. Didn't realize you've never been here, but you did get to see my private sanctuary in Scarsdale."

He slipped his hands away, leaving her feeling empty.

"Follow me," he said, taking her hands in his. "Welcome to my home away from home."

The one thing she noticed was that his home in Scarsdale felt like a home, but his condo had a temporary feel. That was not to say it hadn't been decorated well. In fact, the decorator had done a fabulous job creating an interior that shouted affluence.

Darren kicked the bedroom door open and carried her to the bed.

"I thought that our lovemaking earlier would be enough for me, but something tells me that I'm not going to sleep until I have you again."

The next few days sparked with sunshine. Thursday morning brought the perfect week to an end. Rain poured, but nothing could dampen Eboni's spirit.

Lying in bed, memories of the past few days flashed through her mind.

Making love with Darren was on her list of the most incredible things in her life. She didn't know where their relationship was heading, but she did know that she loved being around him. Since their weekend in Scarsdale something had changed. It was not an overt change, but one that was more intimate, more internal.

It was about her attitude toward the relationship. In the initial stages, she placed no labels on how she felt about Darren...neither of them had.

She hadn't even thought about her sisters for the past few days nor had she had one of her dreams. In fact, she'd slept like a baby. She and Darren had settled into a comfortable routine. Thanks to Captain Ward, who still seemed concerned about her, she'd been granted permission to return home at night. However, in a few weeks, she'd be back to her usual shift.

For now, she spent her nights either at Darren's condo or hers. They were always together. She had to admit, where they slept didn't matter to her—she just wanted to sleep in his arms.

Last night, as with most nights, they'd made love. They couldn't seem to get enough of each other. Each time they made love she discovered something new about his body. Last night, she realized that the area along his spine was overly sensitive, unlike hers, and she only needed to trail her tongue along the area to drive him crazy.

She also discovered that he was adventurous and believed that variety, with her, was the spice of life.

She realized that where sex was concerned she'd been raised a prude. With Darren, each time they made love it was a new adventure.

Last night, he'd brought a tub of ice cream to bed, but when she'd complained about eating so late, he demonstrated a new way to consume it. She could not wait to see what he had planned next.

As she rose from the bed, she mentally planned her schedule for the day.

Darren found the situation amusing, but she didn't. After tonight, she expected her brothers to show her the same respect she had always shown them.

In the kitchen, she glanced at the clock above the refrigerator. She had an hour to eat breakfast and get to work.

She made a quick breakfast and thirty minutes later she was out the door.

As she stepped through the firehouse door about twenty minutes later, the alarm immediately sounded.

"Eboni," the captain shouted, "sorry to ask you to go out so soon, but we have a massive fire on 48th Street. I want you there."

She groaned, but the adrenaline was already pumping into her system. Five minutes later, she was in gear and ready to mount the truck.

The drive to 48th Street did not take long, despite heavy traffic.

At the site of the fire, they jumped into action, each knowing exactly what role they had to play.

"Wynter, you're going in with me," Karl ordered. "There is nothing we can do about the other building, but there's someone trapped in this one." He pointed to the building directly in from of them, its facade barely visible in the thick smoke.

She nodded, unable to speak.

"You ready for this?" he asked, concern in his voice.

"Yes," she replied. "I'm ready."

"Good. Just follow my lead. We have to get this little boy out."

He turned and walked toward a single window with a broken pane.

She breathed deeply. Paralyzing fear slammed her in the face. She sent a short prayer upward and then took a strong step forward.

When she reached the window, Karl had already disappeared inside. She followed him, the heat hitting her in the face, but she knew the window had been the best choice of entry. Thick curls of smoke made it impossible to see, but the light on her helmet cut through blackness and made things easier. Karl's silhouette moved with quick purpose ahead of her.

When he reached the stairs and started upward, she followed him cautiously. In the midst of the crackling and creaking, she heard a voice.

"Karl?" she shouted.

He stopped.

"I heard something. Listen."

He did, pointed to the left and moved swiftly ahead. She followed. At the end of the corridor, flames licked at the walls, blocking their entry into the room.

Karl stopped abruptly.

"He's in there," she shouted over the noise.

She stopped, the heat was still bearable, but she knew they had to act quickly.

Without hesitation, she ran forward, breaking through the flames. Karl followed.

A little boy sat on the floor coughing. He'd had the sense to wrap a blanket around him. Karl picked him up. Turning around, he paused briefly and then burst through the flames.

"Eboni, we have to go," Karl shouted.

She ran through the flames and raced down the corridor. Karl was already hurrying down the stairs.

A few minutes later, she flew through the door, flames licking at her heels, and into the street.

Thunderous cheers greeted her.

She felt an overwhelming desire to cry, but couldn't spare the time. Later, in the privacy of her room, she'd cry. For the little boy they'd rescued, for Marcus, whom they couldn't save, and for her triumphing over the fear that had dogged since the accident.

A man and a woman took the boy from Karl, but the paramedics soon took over.

She walked slowly away, stopping next to one truck, a short distance from where the crew had gathered. She leaned against it. Karl followed, and stood before her.

"You did well today, kid," he said, admiration in his eyes.

She eyed him wearily. "Why did you take me with you?" she asked. "The last few fires, I stayed outside."

"I knew you would be afraid, but I had to make you face that fear or you'd never be any good to me...to us," he replied. "I knew you'd do what you had to do. You were ready."

The tears started to flow, but she didn't care.

Karl put his arms around her.

"You did well, kid. I knew if anything happened, you had my back. We're always afraid, but it's how we handle that fear that makes us good at what we do. I knew the day you joined us you'd be a good firefighter."

She lifted her head and smiled.

"Thanks," she said.

He held her hand and together they walked toward the other members of the crew.

The flash of cameras greeted them.

Chapter 9

Darren slammed the phone down and rose from behind his desk. He had to go to Los Angeles. There was a hitch in the negotiations of a property he'd sold and he needed to be there. He might be gone for a week or more. How was he going to handle being away from Eboni? He wouldn't even see her tonight since he had to leave on a flight as soon as possible.

He turned, picked up the phone again and hit the intercom button.

"Kim, see if you can get me on a flight to L.A. before the end of the day. I can go directly to the airport from here. Call my housekeeper there and let her know I'm coming and what time. You can hire me a car also."

"Yes, sir. I'll get on it."

Five minutes later, she called back to give him his

schedule. "I've sent the documents you need to your *Dropbox* account. Any idea when you'll be back?"

"I'd like to be back by the weekend, but it may be longer. I'll keep you informed."

"Okay, sir. I'll see you when you return. I'll call if anything important comes up."

"Let Roger know that I'll give him a call when I get to L.A."

"Yes, sir. Will do. Have a good trip."

Darren hung up and immediately reached for his cell phone. He dialed Eboni's number but got her voice mail. He left a brief message, explaining the situation and informing her that he would call her later that night.

He took a quick shower and changed into something a bit less formal and packed his carry-on bag. He'd learned that in his job he always had to be prepared.

Three hours later, he boarded an American Airlines flight and waited patiently for takeoff.

The five hours to Los Angeles passed quickly. He read documents on his laptop for the first few hours. He spent the rest of the time with his headphones on, listening to a few of his favorite podcasts. Eventually he drifted off to sleep.

He awoke to the flight attendant gently shaking his shoulder and informing him it was time for the pre-landing procedures. He thanked her, clicked his seat belt into place as she requested and waited impatiently for the plane to land. He'd had enough flying for the day.

And hour later, he was sitting in his office trying to find a solution to the problem that had brought him to Los Angeles.

When he walked into his L.A. home several hours later, it took all his willpower not to immediately fall sleep after he collapsed on the bed.

He picked up his cell phone where he'd dropped it on the bed and dialed Eboni's number.

The phone rang for a few seconds before she answered.

"Hello."

"Hello, honey," he said. "I'm sorry I called you so late, but I just got in. I hope I didn't wake you."

"You didn't. I was reading while I waited for you to call."

"You must be tired."

"Yes, had a hard day at work today."

"Saved any lives?" he said jokingly.

"I did get a little boy out of a fire today."

"You did? How are you doing?"

"I'm good. I feel good."

"I'm glad you are."

"It was a bit…scary. I almost froze, but I worked through it."

"I'm proud of you. Any more nightmares?"

"No, none since Scarsdale."

"That's good," he said. "I miss you."

"I miss you, too," she whispered. "How long are you going to be there?"

"Hopefully, not beyond the weekend, but I'll call you every night."

"I'm glad you called, but I know you must be dead on your feet. Go get some rest and I'll talk to you tomorrow," she said, and then added, "Sleep tight." And hung up.

He disconnected his phone. He really needed to get up and take a shower, but his body refused to move.

He missed Eboni already, missed her more than he thought he would. When she'd told him about the fire, he'd been worried. Her job worried him, but he knew she loved it and he'd just have to work through that fear just as she had earlier that day.

He rose slowly and stripped off his clothes then dropped them in the clothes hamper.

A shower was definitely what he needed, but most of all he needed her. How on earth was he going to sleep tonight without her warm body next to his? He wasn't looking forward to sleeping alone.

Five minutes later, he lay in bed, his arms wrapped around a pillow, thinking about her soft floral scent until he was making sweet love to her in his dreams.

By the following Friday, Darren thought he would go crazy. While he'd chatted with Eboni each night, he missed her so much he wished he could just shut down shop and return to New York.

When he left the office that evening, he felt like going directly to the airport.

He'd finally solved his client's problems and regained some goodwill. Now he could go home. He wanted to leave on the next available flight, but there were still documents to sign in the morning. Then he could hop on a flight and be home in time to hold Eboni in his arms after a late dinner.

Later that night, after he'd gotten into bed, the phone rang. He wondered if Eboni missed him so much that she was calling back despite having talked to him an hour before. The smile on his face faded as he saw the name that scrolled across the caller ID.

It was his ex-wife, Barbara.

"Darren, I've been trying to reach you all day," she said, her tone accusing, as if he'd purposely avoided her calls. She still didn't get it—he worked during the day. He ran businesses and people depended on him to do his job regardless of what was happening in his personal life.

"Yes, Barbara, it's nice to speak to you, too. How was your day?" he asked, forcing calmness into his voice. All he had to do was let her state her case, then he would respond and get the hell off the phone.

"I'm sorry," she said and her apology surprised him. "I'm just frustrated. I hate when plans change. It shows a blatant disregard for anyone involved." She paused, sighing. "I have to leave for New York tomorrow instead of next week. Kenya will be there tomorrow. I hope that's not a problem"

"I'm flying back to New York tomorrow, Barbara."

"You're not in New York?" she asked.

"No, Barbara, I've been in Los Angeles for the past week. I leave tomorrow."

"I'll keep Kenya with me at the hotel tomorrow and bring her over on Saturday morning, if that's okay with you?"

He hesitated. He still hadn't told Eboni about Kenya.

"That's fine, Barbara. I'll see you on Saturday. Give Kenya my love."

"I will do that in the morning. She's already asleep. She is so excited to see you, but I finally got her to sleep."

"I'm looking forward to seeing her."

"Darren?" Her tone had gone serious.

"Yes," he replied.

"Kenya loves you, you know."

"I know. I love her, too. I'm just sorry I missed so much of her childhood."

"You've more than made up for it along the way. You've turned out to be a pretty decent dad."

"Thanks, Barbara. That means a lot coming from you. I'm just glad you are a good mom. If not, I could have really messed up her psyche."

"Oh, you weren't that bad. You just had your priorities mixed up."

"I know. It took me a while to get my act together. If you hadn't left I would never have realized how out of line my priorities were. I've been doing a lot of thinking lately. One of the best things you did was to divorce me. I'm glad you're happy, Barbara. Really glad."

"I've been fortunate. Ted's a good husband and he loves Kenya, but he never forgets you're her dad. He likes you."

"Yes, he's pretty cool. Your taste has definitely improved." He chuckled. "Though, I'm still better looking!"

"Yes, I know. You're still more handsome and arrogant than ever, but one day, you'll find love again."

He paused.

"There is someone?" she asked.

"There is," he confirmed.

Barbara screamed in delight.

"She's a firefighter."

"Wow, that's cool. At least, she doesn't sound like a bimbo."

"Oh, I ended the bimbo thing a while ago. I was just spending some time alone, finding me...and she came along."

"I'm glad for you. Is she pretty?"

"Yeah, beautiful...inside and out."

"I'm happy for you," she said. "Do you love her?"

He hesitated briefly. "Yes, I love her." It surprised him how easily the words came. Once they were out, he felt liberated.

"Then that's good. Don't make the same mistakes you made with me. Though I know we didn't love each other. We loved the idea of being in love."

"At least we can laugh about it now."

"Yes, we can. But I do love you, Darren. Not in the same way I love Ted, but a different way. It's hard to explain."

"I know exactly what you mean. Now, let me go and get some sleep. I have a flight to catch in the morning," he said, and then added wistfully, "I can't wait to see Kenya."

"I have to go, too. Ted is calling. He told me to say 'hi' to you."

"Yeah, let him know the next time I'm in the area— we have to take in a game."

"You men and your basketball!"

"We do have to have something that's off-limits to you ladies."

She laughed. "I'll see you when I bring Kenya over."

"See you."

He hung up.

A wave of dread washed over him. He had to make sure he took care of letting Eboni know about Kenya before she arrived.

As soon as he got home he planned on going over to her place. He hoped this news wouldn't mess up his future with her. He should have told Eboni a long time ago. To be honest, he'd been afraid that his divorce would only prove that the rumors she'd heard about him were true.

He would take her to a nice restaurant, feed her a mouth-watering meal with a wonderful vintage wine and hope that everything would be fine when he told her.

Did she love him? He didn't know. He knew she liked being with him and loved their lovemaking, but did she love him?

He would soon find out. Though not trusting someone was not the same thing as not loving them. Sure, she may love him, but she sure didn't have to trust him because of that fact.

On reflection, he would have done the same thing if she had withheld information from him.

He'd known he had to tell her, but he'd balked at every opportunity he'd had. Now he had to be a man, rectify the situation and deal with the consequences no matter what they were.

He stripped off his clothes and fell onto the bed. He was tired and weary. He needed to get some sleep in order to face tomorrow.

He closed his eyes, but it wasn't until the early hours of the morning that he fell into a restless sleep.

Eboni glanced down at her father. Tears sprang to her eyes. Her mother and her brother Maxwell were outside sitting in the waiting room. She'd left work immediately when Maxwell had called and told her that their dad was in the hospital—he'd had a minor stroke.

She loved her dad, loved his brash, quiet way of doing things. He had been a strict disciplinarian, but there was no doubt in her mind that he loved her, too—he loved all his children.

She'd always felt his love. From that day in the children's home when she'd stood bravely, looking warily at the handsome couple who wanted to take her away from her sisters. But he had taken one look at her and said he wanted her to be his daughter. She'd fallen in love with them instantly.

"Daddy," she whispered in the room that was silent except for the soft, steady beeps of the monitors connected to him. "Please wake up. Don't you dare die!"

Strong arms folded around her. She turned her head. It was Maxwell.

"He's not going to die," her brother said with conviction. "The doctor says it's a mild stroke. It could be worse. He'll just need to take it easy."

She rested her head on his shoulder, taking comfort in his words. She wanted to believe him. Maxwell was the rational one, the one who wasn't always led by his emotions.

"Let's go get something to eat. Omar and Kemar have arrived. They'll keep an eye on Dad until we get back."

She glanced down at her dad, reluctant to leave, but her stomach began to growl.

Eboni couldn't believe how far off track the day had gotten. Earlier that morning, she'd called her parents and asked them if it was a good time to come by. They were ecstatic. But, before she could leave her condo, Maxwell had called with the bad news.

And, today was also the day Darren returned. She was looking forward to seeing him. She realized she needed to let him know she was at the hospital.

She reached into her pocket for her cell phone but it wasn't there.

She'd have to call him later. She wished he were there with her. She needed his presence to help comfort her.

Eboni quickly headed to the elevator that led to her condo, barely speaking to the security men upon entering the building. All she could think of in that moment was getting to Darren.

As she exited the elevator, she noticed a beautiful, leggy blonde walking down the corridor toward her. Since there were only two condominiums on her floor, she had to assume that the woman had been Darren's guest.

The woman nodded and smiled politely, but as soon as the woman entered the elevator, Eboni ran the rest of the way to her door, and after unlocking it, she quickly slipped inside. In her bedroom, she collapsed on her bed.

While staring at the ceiling of her bedroom she wondered why a beautiful woman would be leaving Darren's apartment at that time of the day? While she did not want to come to any irrational conclusions, the evidence was clear. The woman looked disheveled, as if she'd spent the whole night making love.

She walked slowly to the kitchen. She was tired and needed an hour or two to just relax but she was hungry.

Halfway to the kitchen, the phone rang. She turned around and walked quickly to the living room and picked it up.

She glanced down at the number and sighed. She wasn't ready to talk to Darren. She had too much on her mind, and if her earlier assumption was correct she really could not deal with the situation. Right now she had to focus on her dad.

She needed to get out of the house before her scheduled class that night. She would take a run around the neighborhood. She needed to do something to keep her mind off Darren Grayson.

Late in the afternoon, when Eboni left the gym, she realized that she could not continue to avoid Darren. She'd mapped the journey of their relationship in her head and she could not think of anything at all, beyond gossip, that would suggest he was involved with another woman.

The thought of him with someone else made her sick to her stomach. She had to find a quiet place to sit for a while and calm her nerves.

She walked along a narrow path to her home, through the pool area that led to the back entrance of the building. When she reached the small open area past the pool, she was surprised to see a little girl she'd never seen before, sitting on a mat playing with her dolls.

She was reading to them.

The little girl looked up, saw Eboni and waved and smiled. She was adorable.

"Hi," Eboni responded.

"Hi, I'm Kenya," she said cheerfully. "This is Amanda and this is Rena." She held up her dolls.

"I'm Eboni. It's nice to meet you, Kenya, Rena and Amanda."

Kenya laughed. She looked at her dolls and then turned back to Eboni. "They're pleased to meet you, too."

She put her dolls down gently and looked up at Eboni.

"Do you live around here?" she asked. "I wanted to go into the pool, but my dad won't let me. He says I must sit here and play with my dolls for now. Even though my sitter is in the pool with her friends."

"You've just moved into the building?"

She shook her head. "No, I live in Baltimore with my mom, but I'm spending some of the summer here with my dad since school's out."

"That must be cool."

"Yes, I like him now. At first—" she lowered her voice "—he was scary, but I like him now. My mom and dad divorced when I was four, so my mom took me to live with her. But my step-dad is also there and I like him a lot."

"Oh, so you just arrived here?" Eboni asked, curiosity getting the better of her.

"Yeah, my mom brought me over. She's in New York on business."

An alarm went off in Eboni's head, loud and clear.

"What's your dad's name?" Her heart had stopped beating.

"Darren McGregor Grayson," she recited with pride.

"Darren?" she stammered.

"Yeah, and he's handsome, too. My mom told me he has a girlfriend and to be nice to her. I hope she's nice or it's going to be hard to be nice to her."

Darren had a daughter and hadn't told her? And he was divorced?

She felt as if a knife had ripped her heart out. The sense of betrayal she'd felt when he'd not told her that he owned the building surfaced.

"Well, Kenya, I have to go. It was nice meeting you."

"It was nice meeting you, too, Miss Eboni. I hope I see you again."

"I am sure you will," she replied, trying to keep the sarcasm out of her voice. The little girl couldn't be blamed for her father's deceit.

Kenya smiled and waved, returning to her dolls.

Eboni walked away slowly, her hands curled into

fists and her jaw clenched. But her heart hurt—she wanted to cry, to scream. She'd trusted Darren with her most precious possession—her heart—and he'd stomped it with his secrets.

She shook her head, unsure of what to do. So the woman she had seen was Kenya's mother and Darren's ex-wife. She hadn't stayed the night? Kenya had talked about her step-father? This was just not adding up. She knew she'd have to talk to Darren eventually…which would hopefully straighten the situation out.

She needed to trust him, wanted to trust him, but he had to be up front with her. He couldn't continue to keep things from her—things she had a right to know.

While neither of them had given a name to their relationship, they were lovers and certain protocols were expected to be observed if they were ever going to make it to the next level.

She was sure he would have an excuse, one that he considered legitimate and would justify his actions. But she had no intention of letting him think her forgiveness would come easily. If they were to have a serious relationship, he had to know that trust and loyalty, once lost had to be earned again. In the court of love, he would be guilty until proven innocent.

She would stand for nothing less.

Chapter 10

Eboni put the book down, picked up the phone and dialed a familiar number she knew by heart.

Cheryl answered on the first ring.

"Girlfriend, I was wondering what happened to you. You didn't even call me back to let me know how the big date went."

Before she could reply, the tears started to flow.

"What's wrong, girl? You stay right there. I'm coming over."

The call disconnected.

When the doorbell rang twenty minutes later, Eboni rose sluggishly from the sofa. She was so tired. She needed a few hours of sleep before she returned to the hospital.

Just as she was about to unlock the door, the doorbell rang again. As quickly as she could, she opened it.

She almost laughed out loud. Cheryl stood there, wearing a robe that had seen better days. Large pink curlers stuck out from beneath the floral scarf tied around her head.

"I don't know how you got past security looking like that."

"Girlfriend, I know one of the guys who works down there. Just had to bat my eyelashes and he let me come up. Didn't even have to call you!" Cheryl walked inside and closed the door behind her. "The one on duty with him is so hot! I plan on asking him out as soon as I'm tired of Calvin." Untying the scarf, Cheryl pulled it off her head.

"So what's wrong, girlfriend?" she asked. "You're already having man problems? I told you to let me meet that man. I see now, I'm going to have to have a little 'chat' with him. He won't give you any more trouble. Trust me." She pulled a tub of ice cream from the bag she carried. "Kitchen. Now." She headed for the kitchen. "Come on, girl, I'm not standing here all night and letting our Double Fudge Choco Roco melt."

Eboni followed Cheryl into the kitchen, sat where her friend indicated and waited silently as Cheryl filled two big bowls with ice cream. "Now, we're going to have us a good tête-à-tête like *The Golden Girls* over your favorite ice cream—it'll make you feel better. Always makes me feel better."

Cheryl sat, placed a bowl in front of Eboni and the other in front of herself.

"Okay, talk to me, girlfriend," she said.

"I was calling to tell you about my dad."

"Your dad? What about him? I hope he isn't having an affair with a young skank?" she joked.

"No, Cheryl. He's in the hospital. He had a mild stroke."

"Oh, dear. Here I am making all kinds of jokes. Is he going to be okay?"

"So the doctor says, but he is definitely going to have to be careful to avoid it happening again."

"Well, I am sure he's going to be fine. You'll need to get him coming to the gym so he can get regular exercise. I'll bet he spends most of his time sitting in front of the TV."

"He does spend most of his time sitting watching television or reading. I must look into getting a personal trainer for him."

"Good, your father is too young and sexy to be having a stroke," Cheryl said.

"My dad? Sexy?"

"Your dad may be in his late fifties, but, girl, he is still fine!"

"Can we please change the conversation," Eboni said, laughing.

"So we can we talk about the boyfriend now? You still haven't told me about that date with him."

"It was wonderful. We went to see *Porgy and Bess*. The show you and I were supposed to go see. After that, we went on a romantic carriage ride and then dinner at this fantastic new restaurant. The food was exquisite!"

"And dessert?"

"Decadent. We had the most sinful cheesecake—"

"Not that kind of dessert," Cheryl interrupted.

Eboni blushed.

"Girl, you're having sex and still blushing?"

"That may be coming to an end," she said abruptly.

"What you talking 'bout? You're having great sex and want to end it?"

"He lied to me," she said.

"What do you mean he lied to you?"

"He has a daughter."

"Oh, my God. Not a wife, too?"

"An ex-wife."

"That sounds better. Is he still in love with her?"

"I don't think so."

"So what's the problem?" Cheryl paused, holding a spoonful of ice cream near her mouth. "She wants him back?"

"No, she married again."

"I repeat…what's the problem?" Cheryl asked. "I'm confused. The man has a daughter, was married, his ex-wife is married and there is a problem?"

"He lied to me," Eboni admitted.

"How?"

"He didn't tell me he had a daughter and ex-wife!"

"And that's a lie? I'd say he omitted to tell you, but that's not a lie," Cheryl reasoned.

"I don't feel as if I can trust him anymore. He owns this building, too."

"Oh, my God, that's big. He told you?"

"Only when we were in Scarsdale."

"Maybe he was planning to tell you but didn't get around to it. Men are strange about those things. Maybe he was waiting until it was the right time and he knew you better. I think you need to give the man the benefit of the doubt," Cheryl suggested.

"He did tell me he planned on letting me know about the condos, but the time was never right."

"I still believe you should give him the benefit of the doubt. He seems a decent guy. I suspect he may have been worried about letting you know about the ex-wife and daughter. Didn't Maxwell tell you his reputation was a bit tarnished? Not that you can believe everything people say. He may just be wary of all these things," Cheryl said.

"I'll talk with him soon, but he can't think that when he does something like this that I'll just forgive him and everything will be all right."

"I totally agree, but…"

"No buts. Since we are having a tête-à-tête, I have to tell you about my sisters."

"Your sisters?"

"Yes, I'm adopted," she confessed.

"Hell, clutch the pearls. This is a good one. I'm not leaving here until you tell me the whole story."

Eboni closed the door after waving goodbye to Cheryl. Having her friend over for a few hours had taken her mind off the crazy soap opera that had suddenly become her life.

She was heading back to the kitchen when the phone rang.

She glanced down. It was Darren again. She hesitated, and then slowly picked up the phone.

"Hello," she said.

She felt his hesitation, his uncertainty.

"Hi," he finally replied. "I've been trying to reach you since I returned from California."

"I've been at the hospital. My father had a stroke," she said curtly. "And I can't seem to find my cell phone."

"God, I'm sorry to hear about your dad. You want me to come over?" he asked.

"Darren, I'm really tired," she replied hastily. "Can we talk tomorrow? I'm really not in the mood for company. I have to go back to the hospital this evening."

"Okay, I understand. We'll talk later."

Before he could hang up, she said, "By the way, I met Kenya earlier. She is a beautiful child. I didn't even know you had kids. But, there seems to be a lot you haven't told me."

"I'm sorry, Eboni," was all he could say.

"I'll talk to you later." She put the phone down.

She knew she'd been rude, but she was just tired, physically and mentally, and did not want to deal with him right now.

Her main concern was her dad. She knew about strokes and death and she really didn't want to deal with either.

She undressed and moved slowly to the bathroom. Maybe a shower would help to ease some of the tension she was feeling.

She loved her life, loved her family, loved her jobs, but relationships were the hard part.

She entered the shower and adjusted the water between warm and hot. When the first blast hit, it was a bit too hot but she didn't mind. She wanted something to make her feel, because right then she was numb. She knew that feeling something would make her fight, not give up—give up on her dad's health, give up on her job and all the danger she faced...and give up on Darren. She loved him so much but she just couldn't deal with secrets.

What she and Darren shared was too good, too hot, too passionate to just throw it away.

She reached for the shower gel, the floral scent comforting and familiar. She squeezed a generous amount into her hands and then proceeded to rub it into her body. The slow rubbing, deep into a soapy lather, was calming and relaxing.

When she was done she rinsed off, stepped out and towel dried her moist body.

She took one look at herself in the mirror, grimaced at the exhausted woman staring back at her, left the bathroom and headed for the bed.

Within seconds, she was fast asleep.

Darren stared at the phone in his hand before he placed it in its cradle.

He'd messed up royally. But his concern was not for him, but for Eboni. Her father had had a stroke and he wanted so much to be with her, to comfort her, but she didn't want him around.

He knew he deserved it. He'd destroyed the trust that they were slowly building.

Was this the beginning of the end?

If she didn't want anything to do with him anymore, she would be justified. But...he had no intentions of losing her. He would fight. But he would not make the same mistake again. The same mistake he'd made with his ex-wife.

For too long, he'd been on his own. When he got married, he still operated as if he was single. He made the choices and decisions, and only told Barbara what he felt she needed to know. Now he realized that the same thing was happening with Eboni. He needed to tell her everything.

For a moment he placed himself in her shoes. He would be angry, too. He knew exactly how she was feeling right now. He was sorry…very sorry.

The door to the condo opened and Lisa followed behind Kenya who had her two precious dolls clutched close to her chest. Her teenager sitter bent down to kiss Kenya on the cheek, before she turned to Darren.

"We watched a movie and my mom made dinner for us," she said, "so Kenya shouldn't be hungry."

"Thanks for taking care of her. I know she can be a handful at times."

"She's fun and I enjoy taking care of her." She ruffled Kenya's hair. "Well, good night, I have to get back upstairs."

"Again, thanks for taking such good care of her."

"Well, good night. Bye, Kenya."

"Bye, Lisa," Kenya replied. "See you later."

Darren watched his daughter as she closed the door behind Lisa. She was growing so quickly. He wanted her to stay just like she was for just a little bit longer. Her teenage years would soon be upon them and he would have to deal with attitude, independence and boys. He grimaced at the thought.

"Dad, what's wrong?" Kenya said as she came to stand by him. She reached to hug him. "You look sad."

"No need to worry. Just thinking about a problem I have to solve. How did you enjoy your time by the pool?" As soon as he asked the question, he felt like kicking himself. He knew he was about to hear all about Eboni.

"I still want you to take me in, but I know you had work from the office to do so you can be on vacation like me. But I'm still excited to be here," she squealed.

"I am, too," he responded.

"I met a really pretty woman downstairs," she said. "She's really nice. But I forgot Mom says you have a girlfriend already."

Little matchmaker!

"She did?"

"Yes, and told me I should be nice to her. But Eboni is nice, too."

"Eboni?"

"Yes, Dad. Are you listening to me? That's the woman I met at the pool. She's really nice. What's your girlfriend's name?"

"Come, come," he said, trying to avoid a reply. "Let's go get something to eat for dinner."

"Yes, I'm hungry," she said. "I'm going to put Amanda and Rena to bed." She turned to leave but stopped suddenly. "You still haven't told me your girl-friend's name, but I'll soon find out anyway."

She giggled and then ran off to her bedroom.

What was he going to do about Eboni?

There was not much he could do to make things better until he could speak with her and there was no guarantee she would listen. All he could do was tell the truth and hope it was enough. He'd never been a procrastinator, yet he'd put off telling Eboni about Kenya and Barbara—over and over again.

He headed to the kitchen. When he'd finished fixing dinner he waited for Kenya to return so they could eat.

Tonight, he'd see what he could do to rectify his mess with Eboni.

Later that evening, after a few hours of restful sleep, Eboni returned to the hospital. She placed all thoughts of Darren, his daughter and ex-wife to the back of her mind. She needed to focus on her father and his recovery.

When she reached the hospital, her mother was already there. The twins had gone home and she and Maxwell sat outside, giving her mother time to be with her father.

While she had been at home, the doctor had examined her father. She was relieved when Maxwell shared the doctor's diagnosis—any problems her father had appeared to be minor.

"Sis, you want to go downstairs and have something to eat?" Maxwell asked, looking at her strangely.

She was about say no when she realized she hadn't eaten anything but the bowl of ice cream.

"Okay, I don't want to leave, but I know I should eat."

"I know you," Maxwell stated. "You probably haven't eaten since breakfast."

"I ate a large bowl of ice cream when Cheryl stopped by earlier." She looked toward her dad's hospital room. "You're sure he's going to be all right?"

"Yes, Eboni," he replied, taking her hand and squeezing it reassuringly. "Mom is in there with him."

"I just want to be here when he wakes up again."

"I know, but you have to eat or you'll be the next one to be sick. You look absolutely haggard."

"Come, let's go, but I have to go to the ladies' room first. I can't be seen looking haggard, as you call it." She laughed softly.

Eboni and Maxwell took the elevator downstairs to the hospital's cafeteria. They'd made their mother promise to go get something to eat after they returned.

After choosing a meal from the buffet line, Maxwell waited until Eboni was seated before he lowered himself to the other chair.

"Are you okay?" he asked.

"I'm just worried about Dad."

"I know you are. We all are. But there is something else on your mind. Is it work?" he asked.

She lowered her head, unable to look him in the eyes.

"Grayson?"

She didn't respond.

"So it is Grayson."

She nodded.

"You want to talk about it?"

She shook her head.

"I know I've not been the easiest brother to get along

with lately, but you're my sister and I love you. Let me help you," he urged.

"You're just going to tell me 'I told you so.'"

"I might, but I'll still listen. I remember when you were ten, you'd come to me and tell me any and everything. I was your big brother. That's since changed. I'm not sure I like you not worshiping me anymore, but it was inevitable. You are grown."

"It's good to hear you say that."

"I know we haven't had that talk you wanted, but I spoke to Omar and Kemar. We are going to give you your space. Looking back now, I see how ridiculous we were. But you have to promise me something. That you'll come to me anytime you need me."

She could feel the tears in her eyes.

"I promise," she replied.

Maxwell nodded.

"So what's the problem?"

"I think I love him."

"Oh, my God! It's that bad."

She reached across and slapped him on the hands.

"If you don't behave I'll stop talking."

"Sorry, I promise I'll behave."

"This morning I discovered he has an ex-wife and a daughter."

"I didn't find that information when I went searching. I'm losing my skills or they're getting real rusty," he joked.

"Will you stop making jokes about this? If you don't promise to stop, I won't tell you another thing!" she vowed.

"Okay, okay, I promise," he said.

"So he didn't tell you?"

"No," she replied.

"But since you were in a relationship with him, it was inevitable that you would find out," he reasoned.

She paused. She hadn't thought of that.

"That's true. And maybe that's why I won't end what we have. I know what people have said about him, but the person I know is so different from the person I've heard about through gossip.

"He was that person. He gave the press what they wanted to see, but I don't think he ever really liked it."

"I'm going to trust your judgment and give him the benefit of the doubt. You talk to him and straighten this thing out, but if he hurts you, then he'll have to answer to me," Maxwell said in a stern voice.

"Thanks for understanding. So what about you and your love life?"

"Nonexistent. I think I prefer to be on my own."

"That's what you say now."

"Maybe." He shrugged. "But who wants a nerd who prefers to have his head buried in books, does very little socializing and prefers to be at home early on evenings."

"That's who you are now, but before your brief marriage, you were different. You're just scared."

His gaze locked with hers. "You know me too well, little sister."

"Not little anymore."

"Sorry, but you will always be my little sister. Same with Kemar and Omar. I still see them as my little brothers. That's why you all have a big brother like me. I'm supposed to look out for each of you."

"Okay, I won't argue with you as long as you remember, I'm my own woman."

"Fair enough. Now let's eat and get back upstairs."

She glanced down at her watch. "Who's staying during the night? I have work in the morning, so I need to get a full night's sleep. Can Omar and Kemar stay, since they're on vacation?"

"I forgot they have the summer off. One more year and they'll be looking for work. I'm sure Mom and Dad will be glad when they start working and have their own places. Mom has given them until their studies are over."

"Hopefully, work will bring the maturity they seriously need. Sometimes they act like they're still little boys."

"They just like to have fun, but they don't play when it comes to their work. How many other guys do you know that have their master's degrees at twenty-six?" Maxwell asked rhetorically. "Omar and Kemar will. They could have had them earlier if they'd gone straight to college after high school."

"I still laugh when I think of the year they took off to find themselves. Or was it two."

Maxwell laughed. "And we still love them."

They finished their meal in companionable silence then went back upstairs to return to their father's side.

Darren kissed Kenya's forehead and pulled the cover over her. For a while, he'd just watched her peacefully asleep. When he looked at her he couldn't believe he took part in bringing something so precious into the world. He'd had more money than he could spend in a lifetime and yet, that tiny bundle of joy meant everything to him. He'd give his life for her.

He was on his way out the bedroom when the doorbell rang. He moved quickly, but not because he thought the noise would wake Kenya. She'd sleep during a thunderstorm. When she put her head on her pillow, she was down for the night.

At the door, he breathed in deeply and opened it.

Eboni stood there, her face expressionless. She smiled briefly, but he could see it didn't reach her eyes. This was going to be difficult.

"Come in," he offered, stepping aside.

She walked in, looking as if she were entering the lion's den.

He followed her inside, trailing her to the living room, where she stood, her discomfort evident.

When she sat in the armchair, he sat opposite her on the sofa.

For a while there was silence, neither of them knowing what to say. In fact, he didn't even know where to start.

"You could have told me you were married and had a daughter."

"I could have. I could try to find a logical excuse, but I wanted to be honest. I did plan to, but the time never seemed right and I kept putting it off."

"You weren't deliberately hiding the truth."

"No, definitely not. There was a part of me that wasn't sure how you would react, but…"

"Okay," she said, standing slowly. "I need to think about this."

"You are leaving already."

"I need to. Being here—I can't think rationally."

"How is your dad doing?"

"When I left the hospital tonight, he was still sleeping. The doctor says it was a minor stroke. He seems to have a bit of paralysis in his left hand, but nothing that therapy can't help."

"I'm glad to hear he's doing well and you, too." He glanced down at his hands then looked up at her again. "I'm really sorry I didn't tell you about my ex-wife and daughter."

"Maybe this is all for the best."

"How can it be for the best? We have something very special. We have to give it a chance, Eboni. If we don't we'll regret if for the rest of our lives."

"You think I don't know that, Darren?" She closed her eyes and took a deep breath. When she opened her eyes, she looked directly at him. "I'm not promising anything, but I'll think about it." She glanced around the room as if searching for the right words. "I believe relationships have to be built on trust. I just don't know if I can trust you to tell me the truth." She walked to the door, but stopped when he started to speak.

"I care about you, Eboni. I don't take our relationship for granted no matter what others may say. Do you think that you're the only one with trust issues? Trust doesn't come easily for me, either. Maybe that's why

I didn't tell you. Hell, I've gone over it in my head a thousand times and I still don't know why I didn't tell you. I guess we both are going to have to learn to trust, how to be more forthcoming."

He passed where she had stopped to open the door. He then he stood there looking deeply into her eyes.

If he'd only say the words.

She walked out of his condo and stood in the hall-way. It took all her willpower not to beg him to love her.

If he'd only say the words.

But he didn't say a thing and she turned to walk away.

He closed the door with a quiet, final click and then there was silence.

Chapter 11

Anger burned inside—Eboni's words had upset Darren, but he knew that she was right.

He'd messed up and royally.

The past few weeks had been, to say the least, interesting. She'd come into his life at a point when he'd been frustrated and looking for something more. He'd been on a one-way street to self-destruction and being with Eboni had shown him that he needed to rein the wild horse he was on. He was a lot like Rafe, the horse that had been uneasy when he'd purchased him. But while others thought a more rigid training would have tamed the horse, he'd felt differently.

For weeks, he'd just stood outside the horse's stall, until slowly he'd broken beyond the hostility and fear the horse felt.

He remembered the first time he'd seen Eboni. She'd

just stepped out of her car outside his office building. He'd arrived at work and was taking a call on his cell phone.

A group of men at a construction site just opposite had stopped working as soon as she'd stepped out of her car. He remembered what she'd been wearing that day.

The bold red dress and heels she wore made her legs seem to go on forever. He'd noticed her healthy, well-toned body. She was one of the most beautiful women he'd ever seen. She had been a breath of fresh air.

One of the guys had shouted something to her and she'd smiled...a smile that sent an instant, unexpected shock wave straight through his body. He'd decided the encounter was just serendipity and that their paths would probably never cross again. A few days later, however, he'd just stepped into his condo when he'd noticed her getting out of the elevator. He'd recognized her instantly and serendipity turned into destiny.

The next day, he'd done some research at the office and had got the information he wanted.

Eboni Alicia Wynter.

He'd put the attraction down to his lack of contact with those of the opposite sex. He'd obviously been celibate for too long.

And then, he'd seen her watching him from her balcony. He'd felt wicked and daring.

Even now, he could still laugh at the look of horror on her face when he'd dropped his boxers and dived stark naked into the pool.

Now his laughter was hollow. He was in love with her and on the verge of losing her.

* * *

Late Saturday, Eboni pushed the door gently and walked into her father's room at the hospital. Her mother sat upright, asleep next to the bed. Her mother must have been as tired as she was, but the need to be with her father was more compelling than her need to get home.

Her gaze drifted to where her father lay, expecting him to be asleep, only to be startled by two bright eyes staring at her. He smiled, a lopsided lifting of his lips, which took him some effort. Tears sprang to her eyes.

She rushed over to his bedside, took his hands in hers and looked at him with adoring eyes. Despite his condition, he was still the most handsome man she knew. She realized what Cheryl had been talking about.

"I love you, Dad."

"I...love...you...too, pumpkin," he stammered. "Don't... cry."

She released his hands, wiping the tears from her eyes.

"I'm sorry. I'm just happy to see you awake." She kissed his cheek.

"Thirsty," he mumbled.

"Okay, I'll get one of the nurses."

His right hand lifted slowly, indicating a glass and pitcher on the other side of his bed.

She rose, walked around the bed and filled the glass with water.

Her mother woke as she passed her.

"Hi, Mom. Dad wants water."

Tears filled her mother's eyes.

"Thanks, dear. Let me help you," her mother said, rising from the chair and taking the glass from her. "I'll give it to him."

Eboni moved to sit on the edge of the bed while her mother slid the chair closer and lifted the mug to her father's mouth. He sipped slowly.

Eboni looked at her mom closely, realizing that in just a few days, she had aged.

Eboni remembered that as a little girl, she wanted to grow up to be beautiful like her mom. Even with the pain in her eyes, and the cloak of fatigue draping her body, her mother still carried her beauty with elegance. That was the word she always associated with her mother. Delores Wynter was the picture of elegance.

And even now, tired with worry about her husband, her mother's beauty seemed ageless.

"How are you doing, Mom?" Eboni asked.

"Tired, but I'll be fine. The doctor says your dad is going to be fine, but when he recovers, he must take care of himself. We've been talking about retirement for a while, so maybe now is the best time to do it." She held her husband's hand and squeezed it tightly. "We've always wanted to take a cruise around the world."

She pulled the glass from her husband's mouth. His eyes had closed and he seemed to be drifting off to sleep.

"Let's go on the balcony and talk," her mother said.

Eboni took the glass from her mother and placed it back on the table. She followed her mother outside.

They stood by the railing, looking out to the busy street below.

"So what's this I hear about a young man in your life?"

Eboni groaned. She should have known that was coming.

"I've heard he's a good man. In fact, your father and I met him a few years ago when his father passed away. Your dad was his father's doctor. I don't even know if he remembers talking to me at the hospital.

"He was devastated, your young man, but he was strong and brave and I like that in a man. It's not a pleasant experience taking care of someone with cancer. He was hurting."

"I think there is a part of him that's still hurting," Eboni said. "He doesn't seem to want to let a part of his past go.

"I love him, Mom. Why does love hurt so much? I don't know if I can trust him."

"You met a man a few weeks ago and you expect trust to be automatic. Love and trust grows over a period of time."

"But how do you know when it's true love?" she asked.

"When I met your dad, I didn't trust a word that came out of his mouth. He was a playa of the worse kind. A black doctor back in those days would have been a catch for any woman. He had nurses and women of all kinds hungering after him."

"So how could you come to trust him?" Eboni asked.

"Because I saw a man who didn't really want to be that man, didn't want the attention. He just wanted a good life with a good woman. I made him see that I was that woman."

"But Darren lied to me, Mom. Didn't tell me he had a daughter and an ex-wife."

"But you didn't know if he was going to tell you or not. You know what's wrong with the women of today. It's all about quickness and pride. I'm sure he would have eventually told you."

Eboni nodded in agreement.

"When I met your dad, and he indicated he liked me, I made him wait until I was ready. I didn't sit down one day and tell him all about myself. He found out things slowly during our courtship."

"I understand what you mean, Mom. Maybe I'm being too hard on him."

"Have you slept with him yet?" her mother asked.

"Mom!" she exclaimed.

"Just checking. I'm not sure if I want to know, either. You're still my little girl.

"Let me give you some sound advice and I say sound because I'm almost sixty. Having been married for thirty years to the same man and still love him as much as I did all those years ago."

"What's the advice?"

"When you feel that you've found love, go after it. Don't give up so easy and question everything the person does. You'll know the right answer."

"Thanks, Mom."

"Eboni, I love you, the way only a mother can love her daughter. I love my sons, but you are the joy of my heart and I'm so proud of you, I get tears in my eyes just thinking about it," she said. "I saw your photo in today's paper. And I said, 'that's my daughter saving a boy's life.' You went into that fire without a thought for yourself. I know people get scared about death. I know I don't want you to die anytime soon. I want to see my grandbabies from you and that sexy hunk. But if I were to ever lose you while you're doing your job, my heart would still swell with pride as I shed my tears. I would know you were trying to save someone's life."

"I thought you were disappointed when I chose my career."

"Disappointed? I was scared, but when your dad and I thought about it, we knew you wouldn't settle for anything less than what you wanted."

"Damn, Mom. I'm going to cry. That's all I seem to be doing these days."

"Tears have never killed anyone," she stated. "They just help you to clean out all the bad stuff inside that you need to get rid of.

"Eboni, I always told you this when you were growing up...listen to you heart. Really listen to it and you'll get your answer."

"Thanks, Mom."

There was a noise in the room. She peered through the sheer curtains. It was Maxwell.

"Your brother is here to relieve us. I have to go home and prepare for a church event tomorrow. Talk to that young man. He's good for you."

When they entered the room, Maxwell was looking down at his dad. He looked up when they walked into the room.

"Maxwell, I'm glad you're here. I'm going to get Eboni to take me home. You all can go home early tonight. I think your dad is going to be okay."

Eboni looked around the room. During the past day, the mood and atmosphere had been grim. Now there was a sense of hope and expectancy.

When she left for home, she felt happy and alive, as if something good was about to happen.

"Hi, Eboni!"

Eboni turned around. It was Sunday and Kenya Grayson was waving at her from the play park. Eboni's eyes immediately searched for Darren, but he was nowhere in sight.

"Where's your dad?" Eboni asked.

"He went upstairs to get his wallet. Don't worry. Mr. Smith over there is looking out for me until he returns."

Eboni turned around and noticed the security officer for the first time. She waved at him.

"So where are you off to, pretty girl?"

"You think I'm pretty?" she asked. "I think you're beautiful. We're going to see a movie and then go to Ben and Jerry's for ice cream. It's my favorite ice cream."

"It's my favorite, too!"

"Come and go with us. I'm sure my dad won't mind."

"Dad won't mind what, may I ask?"

Eboni's heart stopped. He was standing directly behind her. She could feel his warmth.

"Can Eboni come with us, please? She likes Ben and Jerry's ice cream, too. It's her favorite."

"So what about it, Eboni? I'm sure you don't want to break Kenya's heart."

She hesitated, not sure what to say. Going with them was going to be a mistake.

She turned around and faced him. She could tell he was enjoying this. She was about to make an excuse but when she looked down, Kenya was already holding her hand and looking up at Eboni with a hopeful expectation.

"Sure," she said. "I'll come, but let me go upstairs and grab my purse."

"Oh, goody! We're going to have so much fun! And please hurry, I want to get to the movie early so we can get popcorn and hotdogs."

Eboni turned and hurried toward the building, wanting to get away from Darren and his adorable daughter.

What had she gotten herself into?

She could have said no, but Kenya looked at her with those big brown eyes and she'd melted. That little girl was already learning her father's charming tricks.

Upstairs, she lightly touched up her makeup, added two squirts of her favorite perfume, *Rebel Fleur,* and she was ready to go. She picked up her purse and looked in the mirror.

She was ready for battle. She was not going to let Darren and his darling daughter melt her heart anymore.

"Thanks for inviting Eboni to join us. You like her, Dad? I thought Mom told me you had a girlfriend?"

"How do I explain this?"

He stared down and Kenya and wondered how to explain the mess he'd made of he and Eboni. He watched Kenya's eager little face, and then took a deep breath as he prepared to tell her the truth.

"Is Eboni your girlfriend?" she insisted.

"Yes, she is. But she is upset with me right now, so I'm not sure if she's still my girlfriend."

"You must have done something really bad for her to be upset."

"Yes, pretty bad. But you don't let it worry you. It's adult business and we'll work it out."

"I know, Daddy," she said. "Little children are to be seen and not heard."

"Well, I don't agree with that totally. However, I do agree that kids should let adults take care of their own problems."

She nodded. "But if she likes me, she may like you back," she reasoned.

"Well…"

"I'm back. Thanks for waiting for me," Eboni interrupted.

"I'm glad that you came back, Eboni," Kenya said, a broad smile on her face. She slipped her hand into Eboni's, turned to her and smiled sweetly.

"My driver is already here to take us to the movie. He'll come back for us afterward. I just don't want the hassle of having to find parking." Darren's eyes slid over Eboni, discreetly devouring every inch of her. It had been so long since he'd been this close to her. Too long.

"It makes sense to me," Eboni said, seemingly oblivious to his gaze. "I'm ready when you are."

The ride to the Lincoln Plaza Cinema didn't take too

long. When they arrived, Darren told the driver he'd call him to pick them up at Rockefeller Center.

By the end of the movie, Darren noticed that Eboni seemed to be in good spirits. Unfortunately, Kenya had insisted she sit between the two of them, but during the movie, he'd deliberately placed his arm across the back of Kenya's seat, allowing his fingers to touch Eboni's back. The stiffening of her posture was a clear indication that his touch still affected her. While she pretended to be immune to him, he now knew her indifference was far from the truth.

While he wasn't into kids' flicks, he enjoyed the antics of the characters he'd grown to know so well. Last year, while Kenya was visiting him in New York, he'd been forced to watch the previous *Madagascar* movies with such regularity, he was ashamed to admit to knowing part of the movie's script by heart, thanks to his daughter, who insisted on making watching movies a drama class.

Fortunately, Kenya seemed to have respect for the etiquette of the cinema space and did not insist on her usual enthusiastic participation.

When the movie was over, Kenya clapped loudly, and, of course, he and Eboni were forced to clap, as well. Kenya's only request at the end of the movie was that they return to see it again.

The promise of ice cream was, luckily, enough to put that thought out of her mind…for a while.

When they arrived on the concourse level of Rockefeller Center, the lines at Ben and Jerry's were quite long, so they spent the time listening to Kenya's recap of the awesome movie.

When an elderly lady with her grandchildren complimented him on his beautiful wife and daughter, his heart swelled with pride. However, the daggers flaming at him from Eboni's eyes wiped the smirk off his face.

Of course, his daughter, the child of his own heart, saw fit to show her delight at the comments by giggling and repeating, "Daddy, that lady thinks we make a beautiful family."

Soon, they reached the cashier and his daughter's focus changed to choosing from the vast array of tempting flavors on display.

"What kind of ice cream do you want, Eboni?" Kenya asked. "I want to see if your favorite is the same as mine. Daddy likes chocolate chip buttery swirl."

"My favorite is the strawberry cheesecake," Eboni replied, "but I'm going to try something else today. Maybe the triple caramel chunk!"

"Oh, that's my favorite!" Kenya squealed. "I love caramel." She turned to her father and said, "Can I have a scoop of triple caramel chunk and a scoop of strawberry cheesecake?"

"I'll have the same thing," said Eboni. "I'll try your favorite."

Darren laughed, turned to the cashier and ordered what the girls wanted and added two scoops of chocolate chip buttery swirl for himself.

When their order was delivered and they were seated, Eboni commented, "I can just imagine the calories we are all going to put on. I'm going to have to go to the gym every day for the rest of the week."

"Can I go with you?" Kenya asked. "I've never been to a gym."

"I'll take you a day when there are classes for kids. But I'll have to check my schedule at work first and of course you'll have to ask your dad."

"I know I'm going to love going to the gym if it means I'm going to be as pretty as you when I grow up."

"But you're already pretty," Eboni stated. "Isn't she, Darren?"

"She is. She's the prettiest little girl in the world!" Darren said with pride.

On receiving their order, Darren ushered them to the Channel Gardens, where they stood watching the activities around them.

After they'd finished eating, he lifted Kenya into his arms. She was already drained from their activities and ready for bed.

"It thinks it's time we head on home. She's had more than enough excitement for the day."

"I'm ready to go when you are."

Instead of calling his driver to pick them, they walked to the street and hailed a taxi.

Half an hour later, as the taxi pulled away from the building, Darren handed the keys to Eboni as he held the sleeping Kenya.

"You're going to have to open the door when we get upstairs."

On their way up, Kenya opened her eyes and looked

around until her eyes landed on Eboni. "I want you to come and tuck me in."

"I'm sure your dad will want to do it," Eboni replied.

"He gets to tuck me in all the time," Kenya said. "You can tuck me in tonight."

She glared at Darren, who had the decency to look ashamed, an expression that didn't last for too long when he realized the humor of the situation.

"I have no problem with my girlfriend tucking you in, Kenya." He smiled at Eboni.

"Eboni, Daddy can tuck me in tonight after you tuck me in," she said, before her head fell against her father's shoulders.

Eboni avoided Darren's gaze, which she knew was filled with amusement. Maybe now would be a good time to escape, and then remembered she had to help with the door.

She followed Darren into the building and up the stairs. Darren was sure that if angry eyes could burn holes in someone's body, his would be filled with holes.

"Kenya, go take your bath and get ready for bed. Eboni will be in as soon as you are done."

Kenya then ran off screaming in delight.

"I hope you don't mind tucking her in?" he said.

"Of course I don't mind, but if you think that what you're doing is going to change how I feel, you're wrong."

"Eboni, I have no idea what you're talking about." He feigned innocence. "I hope you had good time this evening. I'm glad that Kenya likes you. At least she didn't have to pretend to be nice to my girlfriend."

"I'm not your girlfriend!" she insisted.

"Then what are you?" he asked, coming to stand in front of her.

As she glared at him, she could still smell a lingering hint of *Acqua Di Gio*. She wondered if he wore it deliberately since she had told him she loved the cologne because it was a perfect mixture of sensuality and masculinity. She loved its aquatic and woodsy aroma.

Now the scent of him stirred an ache inside her. If Kenya wasn't there she would have begged him to make love to her.

He smiled down at her, his eyes ablaze with desire.

He lowered his head and his lips touched hers lightly.

"Daddy, Eboni, I'm ready for my story."

She pulled away from him, turning in the direction of Kenya's voice.

"She's in the room opposite mine. You shouldn't have any difficult finding it."

Her hands itched to slap him across his smug face.

"I'm sure I'll find it," she said calmly. She had no intention of letting him get anything past her. She would go read for Kenya and then go home to sleep alone with no thought of Darren or his toe-curling lovemaking.

When Eboni walked out of Kenya's room half an hour later, his thoughts were still as impure as they had been when she walked in.

He missed her, missed making love to her.

"Kenya says you can come say good-night to her. And, on that note, I'm going home. Thanks for inviting me. I enjoyed myself. You have a lovely daughter. You should be proud of her."

"I am. She'd the best thing that has ever happened to me, and I got a second chance to show her how much I love her."

"You're a pretty good dad. But run along and tuck her in. She's waiting. I'll let myself out."

"Sure you don't want to stay for a nightcap?"

"I'm sure. Maybe another time," she said. "Well, have a good night. And thanks again for inviting me. I had a great time."

"Thanks. You were great with Kenya."

She smiled, turned and headed for the door. From Kenya's room, she heard her shout, "Dad, aren't you coming to tuck me in?"

"Coming, sweetheart," he shouted back.

When he entered her room, she was sitting on the bed, Rena and Amanda tucked under the covers.

He sat on the edge of the bed and looked down at her.

"Did you enjoy your story?"

"I did. I love how Eboni reads. She changes her voice for all the characters. She's funny." She yawned.

"Come, time to sleep, pumpkin. You need to sleep. Remember, tomorrow we have to put flowers on Granddad's grave."

"I miss Granddad. He was so funny."

"Yes, he was."

"But we shouldn't be too sad 'cause he's in a better place and has no more pain," she recited.

"Good girl. So whose turn is it to say the prayer?"

"It's your turn, but I want to do it. I have a special prayer."

She placed her hands together, ready to pray, and made sure he did the same.

"God, if you are listening to me and not asleep yet, I want you to bless Mommy and Daddy and Daddy's girl-friend, Eboni. I'm glad it's her because she's nice and I don't have to pretend to be nice to her. Tell Grandpa Grayson 'hello' for me. I know he's not in pain, but I hope he isn't singing with the angels since he has a real bad voice, but I'm sure you'll find something else for him to do up there. Good night and I will talk to you tomorrow night again. Amen."

The laugh Darren had been holding in erupted.

"What are you laughing at, Dad?" Innocence radi-ated from Kenya's face.

"You know exactly what I'm laughing at." He kissed her on her forehead. "Good night, sweetheart. Love you."

"Love you, too, Daddy."

He tucked her under the covers and walked to the door, then turned the light off.

He was about to close the door when she whispered, "Daddy?"

"Yes, Kenya?"

"I like Eboni."

"Kenya, go to sleep."

He closed the door, but not before he heard her gig-gle.

Chapter 12

Eboni's cell phone rang. She woke, glancing quickly at the clock by her bedside before she picked it up. Just after midnight. Who the hell was calling her at this time?

The Unknown Name, Unknown Number did not help, so she inhaled deeply and picked the phone up. It was Eric Rodrigues, her investigator.

He'd never called her so early in the morning. God, could it be possible?

"Hello, Eric," she greeted, her heart pounding.

"I found her," he said.

"Who?" she asked instinctively.

"Aaliyah."

"Please, say that again."

"I found her. She lives right there in New York. In Brooklyn. She's a nurse."

"Oh, my God. How soon can I see her, meet her?" she said, unable to contain her excitement.

"I have all the contact information for you and will bring it over tomorrow."

"As early as possible. Please?"

"I'll be there around eight."

"I'll be here."

"Bye."

She hung up the phone. She sat up in her bed, staring into the darkness.

When the tears came, they were tears of happiness. She wanted to get up and go into the night to find her sister, but she knew she would have to wait for morning.

"Thank you, God," she whispered into the darkness.

She rose from the bed, wrapped a robe around her and headed to the door. She knew she was making a mistake, but she had to go to Darren. She wanted to share her good news with him.

She opened the door and stepped outside, hoping no one would see her, but knew that the surveillance camera would capture her image. But it didn't matter. Darren owned the tapes.

She walked briskly down the corridor, stopped at the entrance to his condo and raised a hand to ring the doorbell. She paused. She was going to wake Kenya with the doorbell. Instead, she knocked twice and waited.

She'd come to him in a swirling mist that didn't seem quite real. The shadow was vaguely familiar, but as the mist faded, he realized it was Eboni.

She turned and smiled at him, her perky breasts straining against the sheer material of her silk teddy.

In the distance, a harsh sound penetrated the silence, getting louder and louder until he could not bear it.

Darren placed his hand over his ears, but the sound grew harsher and louder.

He closed his eyes, willing everything to reappear, but when he opened them again the mist was gone.

He'd been dreaming, the noise was someone knocking on the door.

He jumped out of bed and headed toward the front door when he realized he was naked and his penis stuck out hard and thick.

He stopped and looked around, finding his clothes on the chair, and quickly put the pants on.

The knocking had stopped but he still walked to the door.

He opened it and peeped outside, seeing only the retreating back of his late night visitor.

"Eboni," he shouted.

She turned around, and ran the twenty meters or more to him, and flung herself into his arms.

Her body trembled and shook, heavy tears falling and soaking his chest, but he did not mind. He welcomed her in his arms.

"What's wrong, sweetheart?" he asked.

"Eric, the...investigator...found...one...of...my...sisters."

"Come. Come inside. You need to talk slowly."

He led her inside, closing the door behind them.

"I hope I didn't wake Kenya."

"No, she's still fast asleep. She won't wake until around seven. Come, let's sit in the living room."

She followed him, sitting where he indicated.

"The investigator just called. He found Aaliyah."

"He did? That's great news. Where is she?"

"She lives in Brooklyn."

"Shouldn't be difficult to get to her."

"I know. He's going to bring all the information to-morrow. I don't know how I'm going to sleep."

"I know you want to see her and soon as possible, but you may need to be careful."

She thought about what he'd said for a moment, before she answered.

"I didn't think of that. Suppose she doesn't want to connect with me?"

"I'm sorry, I didn't mean to burst your bubble. I am sure she will want to see you. Why not let the investigator approach her first and see what she says?"

She nodded this time.

"Okay, I'll talk to him in the morning and see what he says. But you're right, it may be better if he talks to her first and see how she responds."

"That makes a lot of sense to me. Remember, she's not the same girl she was all those years ago."

"That's true," she said. "She may be some gold-digging drug dealer."

"I wouldn't go that far."

"You know what? I don't believe that in here," she said, pointing at her heart. "I know that my sisters have all turned out to be good women. One of the things that kept me going all these years was that one day I was going to see them again. It may have taken me a while to start looking for them, but I know that we're all going to find each other."

"Then, you have to let me help as much as I can. Let me see what I can find out about her tomorrow and then we can talk to your investigator. Let me meet her for you."

"You'll do that for me?"

"I'll do anything for you, Eboni. You know that."

"I don't know what I've done to deserve your friendship."

"It gives me a chance to make things right. I know I messed up."

"You did," she agreed.

"And I apologize from the bottom of my heart."

She stared at him, looking deep into his eyes.

"Can I stay here tonight?"

"Of course. You don't need to ask!"

"I just don't want to be alone."

"It's all right. You can stay," he reassured.

"But no touching. Promise me that."

"No touching…unless you let me."

He watched her indecision before she nodded.

"Good, now that's settled. I need to get to sleep. I've had a hard day with my two girls and I'm tired."

He rose from the chair, took her hand and led her to the bedroom.

Eboni got into Darren's bed, and they both slipped between the covers.

"Does 'no touching' mean I can't put my arms around you?" he asked.

"No, it's okay."

Darren put his arms around her and she moved closer to him. He curled himself around her and she snuggled even closer, her softness comforting.

He closed his eyes, and slowly drifted to sleep, but not before he realized how much he missed having her in his arms.

Chapter 13

Darren looked out at the Manhattan skyline. He loved the city as much as he loved his home in Scarsdale.

He glanced at the clock, its green neon hands moving slowly around its face. It was three o'clock in the morning and he couldn't sleep. Tomorrow, he was driving to Reading, Pennsylvania, to visit his father's grave.

Each year, for the past three years, he'd driven there and each time, the pain lessened.

But, this would be the first time he took Kenya. He was surprised that she'd wanted to go. Then again, she was constantly surprising him these days.

He laughed out loud. His daughter was a trip.

Eboni stirred and her eyes flickered open. She saw him and continued to look. He saw the look in her eyes and he knew she wanted him.

Sadness like none he'd ever experienced washed over

him, and unexpected tears pooled in his eyes. He turned away from her, not wanting her to see his tears.

He'd said before that he loved her, but tonight, he realized that he really did love her.

Loving her had reduced him to tears. The last time he'd cried was at the time of his father's death. Not at the funeral home or the funeral. He'd cried at the hospital when he'd walked into his father's hospital room and found him no longer breathing.

He remembered his cry of anguish had brought the wife of his father's doctor to his side. She'd sat next to him in that room and comforted him until he could see past the pain to make the arrangements for his father's funeral.

She'd helped him to see that his tears were a necessary part of his healing.

He felt Eboni stir behind him, a second before she wrapped her soft arms around him. God, how he loved this woman.

"Are you all right, Darren?"

He turned around, wanting to face her when he answered.

"No," he said, "not by a long shot." He laughed. "My first instinct was to tell you I'm all right. But, how can I be all right, when I have no idea if the woman I love loves me? How can I be okay when telling her I love her scares the crap out of me?"

He almost laughed again when he saw the look on her face.

"Eboni Wynter, I love you. There, I said it and I'm glad I finally said it. You want honesty from me? You want me not to hide things from you? Then that's it. No frills, no fireworks, just the truth. I love you."

Darren looked down at her. She was still, her lips trembling.

She looked up at him, her eyes damp with her own tears. "I love you, too. I'm so sorry that I took all my anger out on you. I didn't mean to hurt you."

He wrapped his arms around her, pulling her to him, wanting to feel her against him. He loved how she felt, loved how the scent of flowers he associated with her reminded him of the freshness of spring.

She raised herself on her tiptoes, running her tongue across his lips, until she paused and nipped him, groaning when his lips opened in response. He thrust his tongue inside, tugging, pressing, sucking, against her.

Darren raised his hands to cup her face, brushing his lips across hers. Her lips were soft and hot. He deepened the kiss, his tongue slipping into her mouth moving seductively against hers.

"God, you taste heavenly," he groaned against her lips.

He nudged her blouse off her shoulder and kissed her neck, her satiny skin intoxicating him with the alluring scent of her. He rained kisses downward until he tasted the sweetness of her breasts. He was rigid with arousal.

He felt her hand at his zipper and soon his pants and boxers fell to the floor. She gripped his penis, gently, boldly exploring his shaft and giggled when it jerked involuntarily in her hand.

But he wanted to taste the firm breasts that peaked against his chest, all the while conscious that his penis was hard in her teasing grip. She was driving him crazy as she slowly stroked his shaft.

He cupped one of her breasts, loving its silken smoothness. He rolled her nipple between his fingers, enjoying the way she sighed and melted into him.

He lowered his head, tasting one nipple as he kneaded the other. She tipped her head back and cried out with pleasure. He shifted his mouth to the other nipple, sucking it until she whimpered in his arms, her body quivering at the intense sensations capturing her body.

When he knew she could not bear it much longer, he slipped his hand under her skirt and pulled her panties down. He parted the delicate folds, which hid a honey inside.

Perspiration dampened her skin as he slipped a finger inside her. She squeezed her legs shut in reaction, but slowly opened them again, this time wider, giving him deeper access to her sweetness.

He touched the sensitive nub, slowly circling, feeling the tension building in her body. She moaned softly as he brushed his finger directly on her pleasure point.

"Darren, I'm so hot. Please," she whispered and her legs clenched around his hand and her nails dug into his back. Her body bucked against him and he felt the sweet warmth of her orgasm.

When her breathing slowed, he eased her back against the wall, tearing the rest of her clothes off with desperation.

He kissed her, his mouth devouring hers as he searched his pockets for that little packet of protection.

When he found the condom, he tore open the packet and rolled it onto his throbbing hardness with the ease born of practice.

He turned back toward her, and moved closer, placing his penis at her entrance.

"I want you inside me," she murmured.

She gripped his buttocks and pulled him toward her until he was deep inside her. The purest pleasure rushed through him, stealing his breath, his shaft harder than it had ever been before.

She tightened around him and he groaned as he tried to slow the orgasm that was riding him hard. He breathed heavily with the effort. He was on the edge, ready to explode.

"Damn, woman, you're so tight, so hot. I can't get enough of you!"

Slowly, he stroked her, his excitement increasing when she rocked against him, undulating her hips so sweetly against him that all he could do was groan.

He quickened his pace, thrusting fluidly into her wet heat. Fire raced over his skin as he stroked faster, harder, deeper. Again, he slowed, fighting the tension that grabbed his body, sliding in and out of her sheath, the friction of his penis against her sensitive walls drew sighs from both of them.

He lifted her, forcing her to wrap her legs around his waist and, still deep inside her, he moved to the bed where they fell forward onto the mattress.

She bent her knees and he recaptured his rhythm with a tenderness that brought tears to her eyes.

"Oh, baby, yes," she whispered against his ear, her quick, short breaths were music to his soul. Then she cried out, locking her thighs around his waist, and moved upward to meet his relentless strokes.

Her release came, hard and fast, her body shaking and shuddering as she cried his name over and over. She clung to him, unable to control the wild pleasure ripping through her body. But he didn't stop. He kept stroking, deep and deliberate, watching her, enjoying her as she shattered in his arms.

He clenched his teeth as his stomach tightened but he couldn't stop the pleasure that ran hot through his body as his orgasm slammed into him. The sounds of his loud groan and her soft whimpers filled the room as he rode the wave of the most intense orgasm he'd ever had. It went on forever as Eboni's sheath gripped him, milked him until he shouted her name, shuddering with his release.

Later, after his breathing slowed, he held her in his arms, and he heard her whisper, "I love you."

The next morning, Darren watched as a tall Latino entered Ebony's apartment. The man looked at him strangely, but when Eboni informed him that Darren was a close friend, he noticeably relaxed.

Without hesitation, he pulled out a manila envelope from the bag he carried and handed it to her.

"Thanks, Eric. You don't know how much this means to me. Hopefully, we'll find my other sisters."

He shook her hand and accepted the small envelope she offered.

When he left, she gave the envelope to Darren, her hands trembling with excitement.

"Open it for me," she said.

He led her to the dining-room table, where he used a letter opener to tear the envelope open.

Several pictures of her sister stared back at her.

"Darren, it's her. Oh, my God. It's her." She rested a palm against one of the photos, her eyes closed. He watched as tears trickled down her cheeks, her eyes gleaming with happiness. "She's so beautiful!"

"Do you want me to call the hospital to find out if she's at work or at home? Her work and home address as well as her phone numbers are all here."

"Would you do that for me? I know I said we could wait, but I have to go see her today. I want you to go with me. I promise I won't take you away for too long."

"Kenya is fine. She'll be with her mother for most of the morning. Barbara leaves today. She'll bring her back in time for us to drive to Reading this afternoon."

"Thank you," she said. "I know you had plans for this evening."

"I'm going to see my father's grave. Kenya wants to take flowers. Would you like to go with us? It's a long drive, but I'd like you to come."

"I don't work until tomorrow evening. Sure."

"Okay, let me make the call to the hospital for you."

He reached for the phone and dialed the number. When the call was forwarded to the correct department, he spoke for a few seconds and hung up.

"She's not at work today," he informed Eboni, watching her eagerness as she browsed through the document in her hands.

"Darren, I realize why it took me so long to find her. She was married—her husband died three years ago. Her last name is now Carrington. She's an E.R. nurse. Can we go now?"

"Of course, I'm ready when you are." He rose and watched her search for her purse, then headed to the door, and she followed.

Since it was Monday, the drive to Brooklyn took a little over an hour. Eboni spent the time talking about her sisters and recounting the memories that bonded them together.

When he pulled onto Linden Boulevard, she spoke aloud each house number, until the car came to a stop outside a simple, but elegant townhouse.

"I have an old school mate who lives in the area. Call me on my cell phone when you're ready. I'm sure he and his wife won't mind if I drop by. You and your sister need some time alone."

"Thank you. I'll call you."

She breathed deeply, stepped out of the car and walked up the cobblestone pathway.

Eboni's hand trembled as she raised it to press the doorbell. She waited, until she heard the sound of footsteps.

The door slowly opened. A beautiful, elegant woman stood before her, her expression pleasant, but searching.

"Aaliyah, it's me, Eboni."

"My Eboni?" Her sister's voice trembled. "Is it really you?"

For a heart-pounding moment they stared at each other and then in the next moment they were hugging and crying and kissing.

Reluctantly, they released each other.

"Come inside."

Eboni followed her inside, immediately admiring the décor as she entered the house. African art and furnishings cluttered the room, but somehow the chaos worked, creating a vibrant, rich ambience.

"You have a beautiful home."

"Thank you. I was lucky. My late husband purchased all this stuff before he died. He was an art professor."

"I was sorry to hear about your husband…about everything."

They'd reached the living room and Aaliyah came to a stop.

"Yes, I lost him after just six months of marriage. He'd just turned thirty when he died. An aneurism. I'm a nurse and I wasn't there to help him. Found him lying on the ground already gone when I got home from work after a night shift."

Eboni walked over to her sister, putting her arms around her.

"I'm so sorry, Aaliyah."

Her sister hugged her back. "It was hard at first, but

I'm okay now. I still miss him, but the hurt is at least bearable now."

For the next hour they talked as if the missing years had never happened.

Eboni glanced down at her watch.

"I am so sorry, Aaliyah. I have to go. I'm going to Pennsylvania with my friend this afternoon. I don't want to assume that we're all of a sudden going to be best friends, but I want my sister back and I'm available when you are."

"I did try to find each of you a long time ago, but I just ran out of money. After my husband died and I received the insurance payment, I told myself that you all were happy and I didn't want to intrude in your lives."

"You wouldn't have been intruding."

"I know that now. Now I've found you, I know that I—we—have to now find Keisha and Cyndi. I'm pretty comfortable now, so I'm more than willing to help."

"Good, we'll talk this week. You have my number and I have yours. We'll definitely keep in contact."

Wispy strands of clouds weaved across an almost empty sky and Eboni stared out the car window. The weatherman had promised a hot, sunny day but the coolness of the car's interior kept the temperature perfect for their drive.

Kenya had fallen asleep after the first hour, tired after singing all the songs she could from her vast repertoire of Disney songs and songs she'd learned at school.

Eboni looked straight ahead, the monotony of the

endless highway was broken up by the occasional vibrant greenery of the towns and villages they passed.

On the car stereo, Darren listened to Darius Rucker sing of the anguish and pain of love. It was one of his favorite songs, which had taken on new meaning, a heart-wrenching depth when he had thought he'd lost Eboni.

He glanced at his watch. They should reach Reading in about thirty minutes.

He looked over at Eboni and smiled. She smiled back, placing a hand on his leg.

"Tomorrow, I'd like you to come with me to the hospital," she said. "My mom wants to meet you. She met you a few years ago at the Harlem Hospital. She said it was the day your dad died. She'd just come from visiting my dad at the hospital. She had just left his office and was passing your dad's room and heard you. She said you were crying."

She could see him thinking, remembering. "That's your mom? Then your dad was my dad's doctor. Wynter? That's why the name was familiar, I had also thought that the association could have been a business connection. The night my father died was the first time I met your dad. My dad didn't let anyone know he was ill."

"How could he keep his sickness from you?" she asked.

"My father was a proud and stubborn man. Maybe he thought he was invincible. We'll never know."

"Were you angry with him?"

"Yes, but his death woke me up to the reality of my

life…that we can party and enjoy the material things in life, but family is the most important thing. Your mom spoke to me that night and it forever changed my life. I was destroying myself. I'd lost my wife, didn't know my daughter and the only thing that was important was living it up and making money. After my dad died, all of that changed. That's why I kept telling you that the man the media knows is nothing like the man I am now."

"I know that. I know the man you are now."

He smiled, reaching over to briefly take her hand in his. "Thank you," he said, releasing her hand and returning his focus on the highway.

There was so much he wanted to tell her, but now was not the right time. He would have to wait until they returned to New York.

Soon they arrived in Reading. Darren drove along Perkiomen Avenue. On his right, he saw the houses on Muhlenberg Street where he'd grown up. At the top of the slight incline, he turned into the Aulenbach Cemetery and parked the car in the tiny parking lot.

They walked to the spot where his father was buried, Kenya walking in the middle holding both their hands. Darren carried the bouquet of flowers in his free hand, which Kenya had chosen at the florist.

When they reached the plot where his father was buried, he stood silent, contemplative.

"Daddy, if people go to heaven, why do they still have to sleep in coffins?"

"Eboni, you can answer that question." He chuckled. "It'll give you some practice."

Eboni laughed.

In the years he'd been coming here he'd always approached the cemetery with sadness and a heavy heart. Today, he felt different. Happiness surged inside, making him feel light and carefree.

Kenya set the flowers on the grave. "Hi, Granddaddy. This is Kenya. I love you and miss you. I'm sure you're up in heaven telling all your funny jokes, so I know you must be happy. Daddy wants to talk to you, too, but I have to go 'cause it's an emergency."

"What emergency?" Darren asked her.

Kenya beckoned to Eboni, who lowered her head to listen as Kenya whispered in her ears. Eboni tried without success to keep a straight face.

"Darren, we're going to see if there is a washroom near the chapel over there. We'll meet you back by the car."

For a long moment, he watched the two people who meant more than the world to him walk toward the chapel before he turned to his father's grave. He knelt and touched the headstone.

"Okay, Dad, I just wanted to tell you that I'm happy now. I found someone who loves me and someone I love. I made it right with my incredibly funny daughter who reminds me so much of you. She has your wit and stubbornness, but she also had your big, big heart. I love you, Dad."

The tears he'd expected didn't come. Instead, he felt a profound sense of peace.

He touched the headstone one last time and walked away.

* * *

Despite the long drive to Reading and back, when they arrived at Darren's condo, Kenya seemed full of life and unwilling to sleep.

However, after a third bedtime story, she'd finally drifted off to sleep. Eboni closed the book and leaned in to kiss the little girl, who'd stolen her heart, on the cheek.

She placed the book on the dresser and left the room, heading to the master bedroom where she knew Darren would be waiting.

Her heart beat faster in anticipation. She knew that tonight they would make love. All day, she'd ached for him and already she was breathless with her need for him.

When she entered the room, the only light was a single candle, flickering on the dresser. The faint light caressed the naked torso of the man she loved who was standing by the window.

Naked or formally dressed, she'd always found him sexy, but tonight, a stark white towel around his waist, the New York skyline, the perfect backdrop, he was the most beautiful man she'd even seen.

As she walked slowly toward him, she noticed hundreds of rose petals scattered across the satin sheets on the bed. She stopped and looked up at Darren. His tenderness, his sweetness, never failed to amaze her. Beneath that hard, ruthless businessman was the most generous man.

He took her hand and pulled her to him. "What are

you thinking? What's making your beautiful gaze so soft and sexy?"

She didn't look away. The time for running was over.

"You," she whispered. "The way I feel about you."

He slid his hands up her arms and she shivered with the sweetness of his touch. "Tell me how you feel, Eboni," he said quietly.

Her stomach dipped as if the floor had dropped out from under her feet. She licked her lips, her throat dry, her heart pounding. "I love you, Darren."

He took her face in his hands. "It's a good thing, baby, because I've loved you for so long that it's become as natural to me as breathing."

"Oh, Darren…" She smiled up at him, so full of love, so full of need and desire.

"Marry me, Eboni. Be my wife and my heart forever."

"Yes," she said. "Yes, yes, yes."

He laughed, hugging her close to him. "You've made me the happiest man in the world."

Taking a deep, shaky breath, then exhaling slowly, she smiled up at the man who made her life complete. "If you think you're happy now, just wait until you get me into that bed…"

Darren arched a brow and then swung her up in his arms. He laid her on the bed, his gentle touch so at odds with the harsh desire burning in his gaze.

"I've been aching for you all day long. Make love to me, Darren."

As Darren tugged on the towel at his waist, Eboni bit her lip, suppressing the moan threatening to escape

her lips. The towel slipped to the carpet. The sight of
Darren's hard, buff body sent a rush of pleasure cours-
ing through her body.

"I love you, Eboni. Forever, baby. Forever."

"Forever," she breathed and parted her legs, sighing with satisfaction as she welcomed him into the
core of her soul.

Epilogue

The wind whistled gently through the trees, while the sweet scent of white poinsettias filled the air. She'd wanted a tropical-themed wedding and Darren had spared no expense.

She glanced ahead to where Kenya stood impatiently. The little girl could not contain her joy of being the flower girl. Her sister Aaliyah and Kenya stood at the gazebo on the large lawn in the back of her and Darren's Scarsdale home, waiting for the music of the steel orchestra to begin.

She was glad Cheryl and Aaliyah had insisted that the wedding take place there and she was sure the guests would immediately know the reason why upon driving onto the property. The gardens, vibrant with color, created the perfect romantic setting.

Eboni stepped forward, allowing her guests to see

her for the first time. The murmuring heighted Eboni's own excitement as she looked across the garden.

"Aunty Aaliyah, Eboni's here. She's beautiful." She heard Kenya say. "She looks like a princess."

Eboni smiled at Kenya and then at her sister. Her eyes stung with tears. For the past six months she'd enjoyed getting to know her sister. Many years had passed, but they realized that the missing years were not all that important. But now was important because they'd found each other.

Eboni wore a wedding gown of the palest blue. She'd insisted that she was not wearing white, but had compromised by wearing a veil of white silk trimmed with tiny blue daisies.

Eboni watched as Kenya put on her most serious face and stepped into the aisle.

Aaliyah indicated it was time, and Kenya walked slowly as she had practiced, tossing white poinsettias onto the ground in front of the couple.

Aaliyah, maid of honor, walked behind her holding Eboni's ten-foot train, but making sure she kept an eye on Kenya.

In the midst of the music, Eboni heard, "Hi, Grandma and Granddad," and Eboni knew that Kenya had reached the pastor and Darren who stood beside him. Everyone laughed, but no one cared about protocol. Everyone, including the firefighters from her firehouse, lined the makeshift aisle, loved Kenya.

She was happy.

Eboni remembered, as if it were yesterday, the stories her mother had loved to read.

Today, she had found her happily-ever-after!

* * *

Later that night, Eboni watched her husband step out of his boxers and walk toward her.

When he stood before her, she spread her legs seductively, knowing he'd stand between them.

He slipped between her legs and teased her, his shaft making her wet with intense arousal.

He entered her slowly, letting her feel every inch of his hardness. She groaned with pleasure.

Once he was completely inside her, he stopped.

"How do you want it, Mrs. Grayson?" he asked quietly. "You want to take a leisurely walk or you want us to ride wild with the wind?"

She reached up, sliding her arms around his neck, and whispered her answer in his ear.

He laughed and set out to pleasure her in a way no man, but he, could.

* * * * *

Her happiness—and their future—are in his hands.

Essence
Bestselling Author
GWYNNE
FORSTER

ECSTASY

ESSENCE BESTSELLING AUTHOR
GWYNNE FORSTER
ECSTASY

Teacher Jeannetta Rollins is about to lose something infinitely precious: her eyesight. Only surgeon Mason Fenwick has the skills to perform the delicate operation to remove the tumor that threatens her with permanent blindness. But the brilliant doctor left medicine after a tragedy he could not prevent, and now he is refusing her case. But Jeannetta is nothing if not persistent....

"*Ecstasy* is a profound literary statement about true love's depth and courage, written with elegant sophistication, which is Ms. Forster's inimitable trademark." —*RT Book Reviews*

REQUEST YOUR FREE BOOKS!

2 FREE NOVELS PLUS 2 FREE GIFTS!

KIMANI™
ROMANCE

Love's ultimate destination!

YES! Please send me 2 FREE Kimani™ Romance novels and my 2 FREE gifts (gifts are worth about $10). After receiving them, if I don't wish to receive any more books, I can return the shipping statement marked "cancel." If I don't cancel, I will receive 4 brand-new novels every month and be billed just $4.94 per book in the U.S. or $5.49 per book in Canada. That's a savings of at least 21% off the cover price. It's quite a bargain! Shipping and handling is just 50¢ per book in the U.S. and 75¢ per book in Canada.* I understand that accepting the 2 free books and gifts places me under no obligation to buy anything. I can always return a shipment and cancel at any time. Even if I never buy another book, the two free books and gifts are mine to keep forever.

168/368 XDN FVUK

Name	(PLEASE PRINT)	
Address		Apt. #
City	State/Prov.	Zip/Postal Code

Signature (if under 18, a parent or guardian must sign)

Mail to the **Harlequin® Reader Service:**

IN U.S.A.: P.O. Box 1867, Buffalo, NY 14240-1867
IN CANADA: P.O. Box 609, Fort Erie, Ontario L2A 5X3

Want to try two free books from another line?
Call 1-800-873-8635 or visit www.ReaderService.com.

* Terms and prices subject to change without notice. Prices do not include applicable taxes. Sales tax applicable in N.Y. Canadian residents will be charged applicable taxes. Offer not valid in Quebec. This offer is limited to one order per household. Not valid for current subscribers to Kimani Romance books. All orders subject to credit approval. Credit or debit balances in a customer's account(s) may be offset by any other outstanding balance owed by or to the customer. Please allow 4 to 6 weeks for delivery. Offer available while quantities last.

Your Privacy—The Harlequin® Reader Service is committed to protecting your privacy. Our Privacy Policy is available online at www.ReaderService.com or upon request from the Harlequin Reader Service.

We make a portion of our mailing list available to reputable third parties that offer products we believe may interest you. If you prefer that we not exchange your name with third parties, or if you wish to clarify or modify your communication preferences, please visit us at www.ReaderService.com/consumerschoice or write to us at Harlequin Reader Service Preference Service, P.O. Box 9062, Buffalo, NY 14269. Include your complete name and address.

KROM13

BESTSELLING AUTHOR COLLECTION

™ CLASSIC ROMANCES IN COLLECTIBLE VOLUMES

New York Times **Bestselling Author**

BRENDA JACKSON

High-powered lawyer Brandon Washington knew how to win. He had to be ruthless, cutthroat and, for his latest case, irresistible. His biggest client, the family of the late hotel magnate John Garrison, had sent Brandon under an assumed name to the Bahamas to track down their newly discovered half sister. He would find her, charm her and uncover all her secrets.

But as soon as Brandon met the beautiful heiress, the lines began to blur. Between the truth and the lies. Between her secrets and his. Between his ambition…and a chance to be loved. And as a storm gathered over the Caribbean, Brandon knew the reckoning was coming. And this time, winning could be the last thing he wanted.

STRANDED WITH THE TEMPTING STRANGER

Available February 26 wherever books are sold!

Plus, ENJOY the bonus story *The Executive's Surprise Baby* **by** *USA TODAY* **bestselling author Catherine Mann, included in this 2-in-1 volume!**

www.Harlequin.com

NYTBJ0313